A Smart Kid Like You

A Smart Kid  Like You

Stella Pevsner

CLARION BOOKS

TICKNOR & FIELDS : A HOUGHTON MIFFLIN COMPANY

NEW YORK

Fourth Printing

Clarion Books
Ticknor & Fields, a Houghton Mifflin Company

Text copyright © 1975 by Stella Pevsner

Printed in the United States of America

Library of Congress Cataloging in Publication Data

Pevsner, Stella.
    A smart kid like you.

"A Clarion book."
    SUMMARY: Just as Nina begins to accept her parents' divorce, she discovers her father's new wife is to be her seventh grade math teacher.
    [1. Divorce—Fiction]   I. Title.
PZ7.P44815Sm   [Fic]   74-19320
ISBN 0-395-28876-2
(Previously published by The Seabury Press
under ISBN 0-8164-3138-8)
Designed by Paula Wiener
Jacket design and frontispiece drawing by Gail Owens
V   10   9   8   7   6   5

jW

For My Daughters
Marian and Barbara

A Smart Kid Like You

# Chapter
1

After about an hour of waiting and watching families, whole families, drive up to reclaim their girls at camp, Nina took refuge in the washroom. Mother, when and if she finally arrived, would just have to look for her darling daughter.

What a mess it was in here! Nina sidestepped puddles on the floor, left over from last night. Some of the more nervy girls had hidden in the shower stalls and squirted counselors who came in to try to control the racket. After a while the counselors had given up. That's when the girls had started tossing rolls of toilet paper from one end of the room to the other, littering stalls and all with streamers. Then they'd gone on to more glorious things, like tossing soggy balls of tissue to the ceiling. They stuck there now like moldy growths. As Nina washed her hands, one of the globs loosened and fell to the edge of the sink. Nina started to put it in the wastebasket but, then shrugging, flicked it to the floor. It made no difference.

She looked at herself in the mirror. Oh, great. The dull brown-blonde hair looked even worse than usual, thanks to the no-shampoo situation of last night. Mother would be so pleased!

And her complexion! Already colorless, it now looked totally washed out from lack of sleep.

She'd tried, these last two weeks, to get a little tan, but what difference did it make? Gram, back in New York, wouldn't know the difference, nor care. She'd put up the money for camp, Nina bet, for two reasons. One, so that Mom could work at the office without worrying about what Nina was doing. She scowled at herself in the mirror. The second reason—and it was just like Gram—was to keep Nina at an uncomfortable distance from Dad. Dad and his new wife.

The door slammed open and Sherry called in, "Nina, your mom's looking for you."

"Thanks."

Sherry kept holding the door open. Nina made

4

her way over, kicking away a piece of paper that caught at her ankles.

"I never met your mother before, did I?" Sherry asked, trailing along the corridor.

"I don't know. Maybe you were out on field trips both times."

"I know I never did meet her. Wow, she's pretty."

Nina gave a noncommittal grunt. She wished Sherry would go away. At the same time she felt guilty for wishing it. Sherry had shielded Nina early in the summer when everyone was bugging her to enter into the *spirit of things.* That was after Nina had told Sherry about the trouble at home.

"I mean, I can't imagine anyone . . . any man . . ." Sherry said now.

"Divorcing her? She divorced my father." Nina tried to keep her voice level. "I told you."

"They always arrange it that way. For appearances. Now, with my mom . . ."

"I know." Everyone knew. Sherry seemed almost proud of it.

"I really wonder how any man could leave a great looking woman like your mother . . . and she seems so nice, too . . . for another woman?"

Nina lowered her voice, hoping Sherry would do the same. "I told you Dad didn't leave Mother for the Other Woman." The very words made her cringe.

"They always say that."

"It's true! Dad and Mom . . ." But why should she have to explain again about the endless arguments, the bickerings? Sherry was really getting to Nina. She'd never write to her. Maybe one dull letter. That was all.

Her mother was standing all alone, wearing a sharp-looking white dress that wasn't even wrinkled. Nina rushed to her, rushed through introductions, and hurled her baggage into the car trunk.

" 'Bye," Sherry called, as they started away. "See you next June."

Nina smiled. That would be the day.

They drove almost in silence while her mother maneuvered the car down the winding, rutted road. When they reached the highway, Mrs. Beckwith sighed and relaxed.

"Glad to be leaving?" She flicked a quick smile at Nina.

"I sure am!"

"I know. I always was."

Nina kept forgetting her mother had ever gone to camp. It was hard to connect this perfectly poised woman to some mosquito-infested spot in the wilderness.

I'll never look like her, Nina thought. At twelve, her own long, strong bones were shaping her into an athletic-looking type. But looks were deceiving. She felt weak. Weak and vulnerable.

Her mother's features and skin had a doll-like perfection. But underneath, those delicate bones were like steel. No matter how bent and beaten she'd seemed after an all-out battle with Dad, she'd always snapped back. During the divorce, she'd sagged a bit, but now, Nina noticed, she looked better than she'd ever looked before. Better than her last visit, even. The summer had certainly agreed with *her*.

"Something wrong?" Charlotte glanced at Nina. "Is my lipstick smudged?"

"Of course not." Was it ever? "I was just wondering. Isn't your hair different?"

"You noticed." Charlotte was always pleased when people noticed. "Antoine convinced me to get rid of the chignon. See?" She turned her head briefly. "He says this cut is more youthful."

So that was it. The soft, easy hairdo did make her mother look younger. It made Nina feel vaguely uncomfortable. How could you feel close to someone so superior? Her glance shifted to her mother's hands, resting lightly on the steering wheel.

"Where did you get that ring?" The finger where the wedding circlet used to be was bare. But this something new on the right hand more than made up for it.

Mrs. Beckwith fluttered her finger. "Like it?"

7

"It's . . . nice."

"*Nice?* Lambface, those are real diamonds."

"Who gave you the ring?" Nina repeated. She knew very well her mother couldn't afford it.

"Mother. Gram. Oh, by the way, she sends her love and wants desperately to see you."

"She just gave you the ring?"

"Well, why not? It's been in her jewelry box for years."

Not enough fingers to wear all her loot, Nina thought with distaste. She could still see Gram's fingers, slightly arthritic, loaded with diamonds, delicately spooning sugar into her tea. And she could hear, in memory, some of the conversation between mother and daughter when they imagined Nina was deeply absorbed in a jigsaw puzzle or book.

Gram hated Dad. Oh, maybe not *hated.* She was cordial enough the few times they met. But she was always making these little remarks like, "Oh, Charlotte, I saw Arthur Schiller the other day. Remember how devoted he was to you?"

That time, Gram had gone on and on. "He's head of a law firm now. So distinguished. And making millions. Millions." Nina loathed the way Gram pursed her lips when annoyed.

"*Please, Mother,*" her daughter said.

Then Gram would go on with something like, "I'll never forget how that man . . . your *husband* . . . won

8

you over with words. Parading all that knowledge before a poor, innocent girl."

Charlotte would argue back. "I wasn't poor and I wasn't particularly innocent. Raised in New York, and those so-called finishing schools . . ."

"Which were meant to prepare you for more than a lowly history professor in a godforsaken town in the Midwest."

Nina noticed that, although her mother defended Dad, she was always more snappish when they came home from a visit to New York.

The ring—Nina wished she could throw it out the window—seemed like a reward from Gram.

"She must be very happy now," Nina blurted out. "Now that . . . that everything's changed at our house."

"I don't know about happy, but she's certainly given me a lot of support."

Support? Nina knew that didn't mean money. Her mother would never take outright cash. *Suggestions.* Gram was great with suggestions. Nina wished Gram would buzz off to the Caribbean or someplace and mind her own business.

She stared through the windshield as rain suddenly beat down. Her mother turned on the wipers. Their sweeping motion was like a taunt . . . *divorced in December, married in May. Divorced in December, married . . .*

"Mother's only concern now is that I'm working too hard. But she needn't worry. My job's going very well, Nina. Did I tell you they put me in charge of research? The company's coming out with a new fragrance . . ."

It was so obvious her mother was purposely changing the subject, Nina hardly heard the talk of perfume and so forth. Why couldn't they ever discuss real things?

She felt adrift. Dad had his new family, and Mother had her new job.

There's no place I really belong now, Nina thought. And all because of . . . of what? Sherry had said the *Other Woman*. But it had started long ago, this moving apart.

Wasn't the Other Woman really Gram?

If Gram was right in saying the marriage had been a mistake from the start, what did that make Nina? Didn't that make her the biggest mistake of all?

During the restless nights at camp, Nina had sometimes courted sleep by pretending she was snugly cocooned back home. But now, after all these weeks, driving again into their once-stately old neighborhood, Nina felt dismayed at her first glimpse of the Beckwith place.

Instead of appearing as a welcome refuge, the house, with its freaky peaks, gables and weather-beaten look, loomed more like something from a ghost story. Even her beloved turret room had an alien air.

"It must be the rain," she said faintly.

"What?"

"I meant . . . I'm cold." She shivered, as if to convince herself.

"Sorry. I'd have turned on the heater," Charlotte said, as they pulled into the driveway, "but it conked out last spring. Remind me to get it fixed before winter or I'll freeze driving to work."

They stopped the car at the back door so they wouldn't get so wet. Pulling Nina's luggage from the trunk, they dashed to the back door. The phone was ringing in the kitchen.

"Hurry, Mother, find the key. I'll bet it's Dad."

The ring broke off before Nina could get across the room. "He hung up!"

"Then call him." Her mother set down a suitcase. "The number's in the phone book."

Nina couldn't. What if *she* answered? Or one of her boys? "I'll wait."

Charlotte blotted moisture from her arms. "I meant to ask. Did he ever come up to see you at camp?"

"He was there once."

"Just once?" Her look seemed to say *Hah!*

"They . . . uh . . . went somewhere. Before that, Dad taught summer school."

"I hope he wrote to you, at least?"

"Sure, he wrote." Long, beautiful letters, which never made mention of the fact that her own were curt. Nina picked up a suitcase and started down the hall. Her mother, following, persisted, "Did he come alone when he visited you?"

"Yes."

"So you've still never seen the new . . . seen Dolores?"

"No." She wished her mother would stop this.

"She's not much to look at. But then, I guess she has other qualities."

"Mom!" Nina stopped at the top of the winding stairs. "What have you done to my turret room?"

"Nothing. Just stored some things in there. Do you want it cleared?"

"I'd like it back."

"All right, then. I'll move the stuff into the study down the hall. He finally hauled away the last of his junk."

It wasn't junk. Nina's father had kept shelves full of books and scholarly journals in the study upstairs, where he could work undisturbed. This stuff in the turret room was more like junk. Fashion and decorating magazines and hunks of fabric. Her mother was always redoing things whether they could afford it or not.

"Don't worry about it now," Charlotte said, as

Nina nudged a roll of wallpaper with her foot. "You'll have your precious room back. Maybe we could fix it up like . . . like something from the *Arabian Nights*? With these high ceilings?"

"Mother, I'm beyond fairy tales." Nina didn't want it *fixed up*. The turret room was a thinking place, not a show place. "But thanks, anyway," she added.

"You'll be glad to know your bedroom's exactly as you left it. I'm going to change out of these clothes."

With her mother out of the way, Nina went down the hall and looked into her Dad's old study. It had been a bedroom when this house had held the original Beckwith family. Did houses retain the spirits of people who had lived there, Nina wondered. If so, what were these empty walls feeling? Did they resent the fact that this house had come into the hands of a Beckwith-by-marriage-only? She closed the door. Across the hall was a smaller room, also vacant except for furniture. They'd always had a college girl during school terms who helped around the house in exchange for room and board. But after that born loser, Linda, last year, Nina wondered if there'd be another this fall.

She was back in her room, halfheartedly unpacking, when she heard the phone ring down the hall in her mother's room.

"Nina, it's for you."

"Is it Dad?" She felt a thud in her chest as she went toward the phone.

"No. Angie."

Within a few seconds she was back to old times, with Angie carrying on in that familiar bubbly voice of hers.

"I can't believe it! I can't believe you're actually back! Oh, guess what . . ." And the talk went on for at least a half hour. Naturally, Angie didn't once mention her brother—why should she? And Nina couldn't think of any way to bring his name into the conversation. Tom. The very thought of him gave Nina goose bumps. But she'd die if anyone knew! Finally, Mrs. Beckwith, who had gone downstairs, picked up the extension and asked Nina to come down to eat.

"Be sure," Angie said, before hanging up, "to look through the mail for your schedule. You've gotta have it in junior high or you can't move. Except to the office." She made an *uk* sound. "Phone me back right away."

"I've got to wait for a call from my dad."

"Then right after he calls, call me. Promise?"

As the evening wore on, Nina waited at first nervously, then impatiently, and finally with a depressing *knowing*.

Dad wasn't going to call that night.

At about ten o'clock when she went into her mother's room to say good-night, wondering if she ought to call back Angie this late, the phone rang. Nina snatched it. "Hello?"

"Oh. Nina?"

She felt strange. "Dad . . . ?"

The voice cleared. "No. Uh, this is Phil. Is your mother home?"

Nina handed the phone over. "It's someone named Phil."

Her mother, with a half-embarrassed little smile, took the phone, but before saying anything reached over and kissed Nina's forehead in dismissal. "Good night, darling," she called, as Nina walked across the room. Nina turned, and her mother, still waiting, blew a kiss.

Nina softly shut the door, but before the *click*, her mother's voice filtered through. "Hello, darling," she was saying.

Nina went to her room and closed that door with a slight slam.

# Chapter 2

Nina turned off her alarm and burrowed back into the covers. It was too much to get used to all at once. Being home after a whole summer away at camp, getting used to the fact all over again that Dad was gone and would never live in this house with her again, and then starting school today. The very first day after getting home.

The rain, still coming down, made the room gray as a ghost. Nina leaned over to turn her bedside radio to rock and also to flick on a lamp.

If Mom's gone to work already, she thought, I'll just stay in bed. Pretend the alarm didn't go off. *Junior high.* The very thought brought a searing pain to her middle. If it were just a little more to the right . . .

"Nina!" Her mother rattled the door open. "Aren't you up? Get moving, I haven't time to fool around with you."

"I may have appendicitis."

"Turn that junk down," her mother said. "I can't hear a word." Which didn't make sense, because she left anyway.

Later, in the kitchen, Nina moved her mother's coffee pot out of the way and put the makings of hot chocolate into a pan. While it heated, she dialed the familiar number.

"Hi!" Angie squealed. "I almost called back anyway last night. What happened?"

"I'll explain later. I have my schedule here if you want to check classes."

"Sure. Hang on a second."

"For heaven's sake," Mrs. Beckwith said, coming into the room, "why are you wasting time . . . ?"

Nina grabbed the cocoa pan, which was about to boil over. Angie's voice said, "I've got it. First class is . . ."

"Angie, could you hold on a second?" Nina turned to her mother. "You leaving?"

"I'd like to, if you could get disconnected."

"Angie? Hold on, will you?" Nina turned again to her mother, who was visibly irritated.

"Here's the house key," she said, putting it on the table. "Be sure to lock up before you leave. And Nina . . ." her eyes behind the makeup and brambly lashes looked troubled. "I'll try to be home early. In the meantime, don't let anyone you don't know into the house."

"Mom, you're always like this when you've been with Gram. You'd think there were all kinds of muggers . . ."

"Just do as I say, please. And here's money for lunch. I'm sorry to rush off like this. Tonight we'll go over the list of supplies you need. And clothes. Good heavens, Nina, don't you have a shirt that's ironed?"

"I like this one." Nina could hear little sounds from the phone against her chest. "Besides, it doesn't matter in this weather. Oh, Mother, drive carefully." Hint, hint.

As Nina lifted the receiver, she heard strange animal sounds and the words, "Help, I'm trapped in a telephone cord! Get me out!"

"Hold on just a second."

"Hold on?" Angie wailed. "I'm losing my grip . . . I'm slipping . . . slip . . . ping!" Her voice trailed off.

"Can't you do your talking on the bus?" her mother asked.

"We haven't said anything yet!" Nina protested. She glanced at the clock. "Angie," she said, "I'm sorry, but I've got to hurry. I catch the bus before you do."

"Three minutes before. Okay. Save me a seat." Angie hung up.

"I'm off the phone," Nina said. She poured the chocolate, which was too hot to drink now.

"Honey, don't be annoyed," her mother said. "I just want to make sure . . ."

"I'll catch the bus all right. I'm not a baby."

"You're still my baby."

Nina poured water into the mug of chocolate to cool it. She kept her back toward her mother.

"Good-bye then, pet. See you tonight." Nina felt the nearness and the lips brushing her hair.

" 'Bye," she muttered, not turning around. Nina stood motionless until she heard the car pull out of the garage. Then she rushed upstairs to brush her hair and get her purse and things and then back to the kitchen to snatch up her schedule.

She barely made it to the stop before the bus came barreling down the street, sluicing sheets of water toward the curb. In the few seconds it took to get her umbrella slammed shut, she had the feeling that every kid in the bus was gawking at her through the misty windows.

Inside, she paused. "Seats at the back," the driver said impatiently, hand on the gear shift.

Nina lurched down the aisle, trying to keep from stumbling over feet stretched out in the aisle.

"Hey, honey, want to sit here?" A boy with a school jacket zipped to his chin deliberately blocked her way.

"Aw, she doesn't go for you, Thompson," the boy across the aisle said.

Nina edged past and slid into a seat. There probably wasn't one kid she knew. She dreaded the thought of riding with this bunch every day, especially if they found out she was from the university school. She fished a scarf from her raincoat pocket and wiped the steamy window.

At about the third stop, a shout went up from the big-mouthed boy as a group of kids got on. "Rafferty! Hey, boy, how many baskets you gonna sink this season?"

Nina took a deep breath as she saw Angie's brother at the front of the bus. He was taller and better looking than ever, but his smile was full of metal.

"It's Brace Face!" the kid across the aisle shouted. "When did they wire you, boy?"

Tom kept on smiling as he walked past Nina, toward the back of the bus. He hadn't noticed her. But then, he never had. It wasn't that he was jealous because Nina and his sister had attended the university school. Even if he'd passed the aptitude test, Tom would have kept right on at the regular school with its all-out sports program.

Angie, who was not only miles shorter than her brother but shorter than most kids, finally bobbed into view. Nina waved and Angie stumbled back, giggling at the suggestions that she join the boys.

"Oh, ish," she said, dropping into the seat beside Nina. "I feel like a tadpole. Hey, I can't believe you're really back!" She ran two fingers along her dark, dripping hair, stripping off water. "I was afraid at the last minute you wouldn't be on the bus." She wiped her eyes as though she had just surfaced from a dive. "Or that I wouldn't recognize you after all these weeks. Aren't you scared?"

"Of what?" Nina asked.

"Of getting lost in the new school. They just barely got it built in time. And it's huge. It'll be a riot, everyone running around like crazy. Even the eighth graders will be as loused up as we are. And the teachers."

"Let's quick compare schedules," Nina said, taking hers from her pocket. "Maybe we can stick together."

They held the cards side by side.

Angie ran her finger along the lines. "Homeroom, that's English, too, together. Then . . ." She zigzagged back and forth. "Not again until science.

Science. I wonder if they put a red alert on my file card after what happened last year."

"You didn't actually blow anything up," Nina said. "Look, we have lunch hour the same time."

"But then nothing again until last period math. It's a rotten conspiracy. Do you suppose they did it deliberately? Separated the experimental kids?"

"I don't know." It wasn't a happy thought. Big new school, strange classmates, and a whole pack of untried teachers. Instructors who couldn't care less that she was the daughter of Professor Beckwith. "Are junior high teachers pretty tough on the students?" Nina asked.

"Tom says it all depends," Angie replied. "There'll be a lot of new ones because of the two junior highs now."

The noise in the bus rose to a roar. They had arrived at the new building. Other than being new, it looked awful. Two flat floors of windows and bricks, like an institution. And outside, bunches of ugly construction trucks parked near mounds of dirt.

Kids streaked toward the school's entrance, deliberately sloshing through puddles. One of the doors, blocked off with a sawhorse, carried the message *W e t P a i n t.*

"Wet *paint!*" Angie howled. "Wet everything. Come on, guys, push on and get under cover."

Inside, the only thing that looked halfway decent

was a rocked-in area of plants under a skylight. The hall seemed to be wide enough for a herd of elephants. And even though the walls were painted a supposedly cheery yellow, anyone could see they were built of coarse concrete blocks.

Overhead, a voice from a loudspeaker rasped: *Incoming students, please do not loiter by doors. Proceed immediately to your lockers. I repeat, move immediately to your lockers.*

Where are our lockers? Nina wondered. The crowd pushed them down the corridor to the left. The new floors were getting all slopped up from wet shoes.

After a slight jog in the wall, the lockers loomed up. Nina edged to the right. "Mine should be here close," she said to Angie. "It's number 44."

Static overhead. Then: *A warning bell will be sounded in five minutes. You are to proceed to your homeroom in an orderly manner.*

"Gotcha, chief," Angie said, saluting toward the ceiling. "Any more orders?"

The voice zapped: *At the end of three minutes, after the warning bell, you are to be in your homeroom.*

"I wonder how we're supposed to find our home room," Nina said.

"It's upstairs—201. Let's both of us dump our coats into your locker and proceed immediately. We'll meet back here after school."

They did and started down the hall.

I repeat: A warning bell will be sounded in five minutes. . . .

Over the sound of the loudspeaker, Angie said in a guttural voice, "And anyone caught loitering will be swiftly brought to trial and exterminated." She squashed an imaginary bug with her heel. "And now an important message: Students, why suffer the misery of back-to-school migraine . . . ?"

Nina tugged at Angie's sleeve. "That sign points up for rooms 200 and so forth. And there's the stairs."

At the stairway, a sign said *Down Staircase.*

Angie giggled. "What a riot! Tom said it would be like this. They chase you all over the building to wear down your resistance."

"I wish Tom had come along," Nina said. And then quickly, "As a guide."

"Are you kidding? He said if I met him in the hall not to even let on that I know him. What an insult." Angie laughed and flicked back her hair. "Besides, what does he know? Hey, that way must be the stairs."

As they trudged up the *Up Staircase,* Angie commented, "With our luck, Room 201 will be down at the other end of the hall. But at least with all this action I'm drying off."

At the head of the stairs a snappish-looking girl with a student badge pointed out the way to 201.

"They station these kids around," Angie explained, as they headed down the hall, "to see that no one goes the wrong direction on the stairs or runs around without a pass between classes."

"What if you do?"

"The hall monitor rats on you. And you get a detention."

"Kept after school?"

"Right. There's Cheryl. Hey, Cheryl!"

If Nina were kept after school, she'd miss the bus. And there was no Dad to drive her.

With Cheryl, they wandered to the back of Room 201 to give great, excited greetings to a handful of others from the university school. After the first hellos, Nina felt Cheryl and Sandy eyeing her. They know about Dad getting married last May, Nina thought. They're wondering how I'm taking it.

"Hey, guys," Angie said, "did you ever track down that owl in the tree?"

The girls' eyes flicked to Angie, and they broke into howls.

"We knew it was Bart!" Cheryl squealed.

"Sure. His mother told my mother they were looking all over the neighborhood for him. Almost called the cops."

"What was it? A slumber party outside?" Nina asked.

"Yeh, you really missed it," Sandy said. "Were you actually at camp the whole entire summer?"

"I was."

"Don't say another word until you've talked to your lawyer," Angie muttered. She'd meant to be funny, but at the word *lawyer,* they all got secretive looks.

"I have nothing to hide," Nina said with a touch of defiance. She wasn't going to pretend. Not this year.

At the sound of the bell the kids scooted into seats. The teacher turned from the board where she'd written *Miss Primrose,* a name that didn't seem to suit her. She looked lively, not prim, and more like a carrot than a rose. She was tall and skinny and had red hair piled on top of her head. Some of the strands frizzled around her freckled cheeks.

"Welcome to Fremont Junior High," she said. "We really ought to have a ribbon-cutting ceremony, but let's just call roll instead." She picked up a clipboard. "As you may know, this is your homeroom as well as your English class. If you have any problems, feel free to stop by and I'll try to help you out."

She went through the roll call, scribbling in pronunciation helps on her list. Nina counted only eight kids from the old school. Quite a change from the old days when one new kid was a big event.

Miss Primrose lost no time in passing out textbooks and plunging everyone right into a survey of the semester's work. To top it off, she dashed off an assignment to a background of complaints. Angie loaned Nina a pen and sheet of paper so she could copy the assignment. *See you in science,* she'd scribbled at the top of the page.

In study hall, in spite of the noise, Nina finally managed to concentrate on the lit work. Then she thumbed through to an excerpt from *Jane Eyre.* Reading was fun when you didn't have to stop and analyze every other sentence. She bet some of those authors would die laughing (if they hadn't been dead already) at how every little thing they wrote was supposed to be *significant.*

After science, when they'd located the lunchroom (mostly by the awful smell of macaroni and cheese), Angie asked, "Are there any cute boys in your classes?"

"Lots," Nina said. She'd have to start noticing. (She hadn't caught one glimpse of Tom all morning.)

What she mostly noticed that afternoon was the great number of new faces. When there was someone she knew, she'd sit near her. Then, at the last period of the day, Nina's spirits revived. Before she even got to the math room, she knew it was going to be class reunion time.

"Isn't this great?" Angie said, popping up from nowhere. "Practically every kid we know is headed for 101. I guess old Sherwood did what he said he was going to do. Landed us all in Accelerated Math."

The commotion was unbelievable. Worse than study hall. The campus kids, never known for their reserve, were living up to their reputation. There was no teacher around to jump on them or to appeal to their sense of maturity.

She (for some reason Nina had been thinking the teacher would be a man) came bustling in now, like a boat sailing through churning seas. She didn't even tell them to cut the racket or anything. Just headed for the desk, pink-cheeked and out of breath.

So far, she was the most cheerful looking teacher Nina had seen all day. Small and snappy, with close-cropped hair and an impish smile, she could almost have worn jeans and gotten by with it.

"I take it I'm in the right place." The teacher dumped a pile of stuff onto the desk. The class, out of curiosity, quieted.

"They have me flying from room to room like a jaybird," she said conversationally. "Worse than a college campus. Almost." She smiled at the kids up front. "You're seventh grade Accelerated Math? All of you? Big class. But we won't have any problems."

"Good," someone said.

She laughed. "You might as well know this is my first year of teaching after an absence of some years. I'm really flattered that they assigned me this class because I'm told you're all whizzes in math. I expect to have a lot of fun."

She'd better have a lot of courage, Nina thought. These kids, given a chance, could drive a teacher right up the wall. Old Sherwood almost hit a kid one day last year. But this Miss—whoever she was—just might be able to handle the group. Under that dark-eyed, dark-haired freshness, there was a wise old don't-push-me-too-far kind of look.

"I say fun because I think of math as a series of puzzles to solve," she continued, leaning against the desk. "I'll give you the clues in class and then turn you loose to come up with solutions. You can work at your own speed and check in with me to see if you're on the right track. With this method, there's very little homework. Outside of class, I'm sure you have better things to do with your time. I know I have."

Nina looked at Angie, and they waggled their eyebrows in agreement. This class was going to be a snap.

Angie ducked her head and mouthed the words, "Wait for me at your locker."

Nina was about to ask, *Can you come over later?* when the teacher's words stopped her cold.

"I guess I forgot to tell you. My name's Mrs. Beckwith."

The class was totally silent. Then someone said, "What?"

"Mrs. *Beckwith.* Want me to spell it?"

As several kids turned around and curiously eyed Nina, she felt the teacher's gaze on her. The woman glanced away almost immediately and turned toward the desk. "Let's pass out these books and get going," she said. "You people at the front pick them up."

Trembling, not yet believing this could actually be happening, Nina waited until Cheryl, the last one to give a lingering look, finally turned away. Then she raised the cover of her lit book and slid out the schedule card.

There they were: all the classes, all the room numbers, and all of the teachers' initials.

Nina's eyes were blurring a little, but those last initials stood out black and clear: D.B.

D.B. Dolores Beckwith. *Her!*

 Chapter
3

Nina felt absolutely paralyzed. She was aware of certain bodies still twisting around to look at her and an undercurrent of whisperings.

As if in a haze, she heard the teacher's voice talking about roll call. She knew another bad moment was coming up.

The woman started reading off names. "Hank Anderson? Fine. You prefer Hank to Henry?" She made a note. "Kim Bailey? Is Kim here? Oh, there you are." Another check mark. One more name and then, "Nina?" Slight hesitation. "Nina Beckwith?"

What a beast! Nina would not raise her hand. But she was forced to look.

The woman met the look head on. "All right," she said. She lost her place for a moment, the first sign she'd given of being the least bit shook. After that she took her time, commenting on names and kidding a little.

Gradually, the stiffness drained away in Nina, leaving a numb, trapped feeling. She glanced at Angie. Angie turned slowly toward her, her eyes rounded and her look full of helpless sympathy. Nina forced a shrug. There was nothing to do. A kid couldn't just get up and walk out of class. Her legs felt limp anyway. She'd never make it to the door.

But once sprung, she knew she'd never come back to this class again. They couldn't make her. No school in the world could force her to come back to this room with this woman. It was barbaric. Stealing away someone's father and then capturing his daughter in class.

I hate her looks, Nina thought. I hate the way she's playing up to the kids, pretending to be such a winner. I hate the principal for letting her take over this class. I hate this school.

They were passing out books now, with the woman kidding around, making a play for laughs.

Kevin turned to give Nina her text. She snatched it out of his hand and glared so he turned right around.

"Let's skip to page 73," the woman said. "Up until there it's mostly review, which I doubt any of you need." Another plug for popularity.

Nina left the book lying but, afraid of calling any more attention to herself, finally opened it and riffled through, ripping a page.

The creeps, putty in the hands of this woman, were trying to outdo each other to show off their brilliance. Nina hated them too, the no-loyalty bunch!

The sounds of the class became a blur as Nina sorted over possibilities of what to do. She could call her father and lash out at him for this thing that was indirectly his doing. But she'd been out of touch with him too long. He might have changed. Or worse, he might want to get together with that woman and Nina for a three-way discussion. That was out. O-U-T.

To appeal to Mother was a deadly idea. She wouldn't stop to talk. She'd act. She'd yank Nina right out of this class. Or maybe out of this school. Oh, boy! And where would she send her? To Gram, Nina bet. Double O-U-T.

Darn this school! And the principal. Didn't he have any sense of decency when he assigned the pupils? But Nina knew, despite her feeling of rage, that this class had been assigned as a group. The school might even use a computer, making her no more than a card in an index file.

Wasn't there anyone, though, who could get her out of this mess?

Miss Primrose.

"Any little problems or conflicts . . . If so, I'll try to help you out." That's what she'd said.

I'll dash right up there after class, Nina thought. And tell her . . . tell her . . . I don't want to be in Accelerated Math. Let her think I'm a scared student. I don't care what she thinks.

Finally the class ended.

Although it was Nina's aim to shoot right out of the room, being in the back, she had to maneuver.

Mrs.—the woman—glanced up from her jolly remarks to give Nina a look that said *please wait.* Nina looked away and cut around Rose Hawkins who was, as usual, putting out with her famous oh-this-is-going-to-be-so-stimulating slush.

In the hall, Angie caught Nina's arm. "Get my coat and save a seat on the bus," she ordered.

Nina was only too glad to get away from the appraising looks of Cheryl, Sandy, and one or two others. Still, she said in an undertone, "I want to find Miss Primrose."

"Don't," Angie said. "Tell you why later."

Nina stood indecisively for a moment. But as the kids clustered around Angie down the hall a little way, Nina turned and went toward her locker. She could see

34

Miss Primrose in the morning possibly. After she found out what Angie was cooking up.

She got nervous in the bus, afraid Angie would miss it. But at the last minute, while the motor was turning and the bus beginning to vibrate, she came tearing through the late afternoon mist.

As she hustled down the aisle, kicking at careless feet, Angie's face was triumphant. Several kids elbowed her.

"Isn't this a riot?" Angie said, returning a punch to a kid across the aisle before sliding into the seat next to Nina. "I'm a mass of bruises, I bet."

"What was all that about inside?" Nina asked. "With the kids?"

"Oh, wow, wait'll I tell you!"

"And what about Miss Primrose?"

"She's the last person here you should go running to with your troubles. Didn't you see her at lunch with Mrs. You-Know-Who?"

"I didn't . . . notice."

"Well, I did. And they had that old-friend look. You know, not superpolite, just comfortable and laughing."

Laughing. Nina shuddered at her narrow escape. She could imagine the school staff in the teacher's lounge, talking about her and the family situation and comparing notes on how she seemed to be taking it.

Before the bus even got out of the parking lot, the bus driver shifted into neutral and twisted to tell a few kids to cut out the roughhousing or get out and walk. It had begun to rain once more.

When they got going again, Angie put a notebook up to her mouth and Nina's as a shield. "The reason I wanted you to go on ahead was so I could talk to the kids without getting anyone suspicious," she murmured. "In case You-Know-Who came charging out of the room."

"But what did you want to talk about? I mean, what good could it do? The kids thought it was just hysterical. I could tell from the way they were looking at me."

"That's where you're wrong. They're as ticked about this whole thing as you are."

"Really?" It didn't seem very likely.

"Sure they are. You know how our class always sticks together."

"Well . . ."

"And there's no stopping that bunch once they decide to drive a teacher up the wall."

Nina was beginning to feel better. "Is that what they decided to do?"

"Naturally."

"But they like her. I could tell."

"At first, maybe. But they're not going to let her

get by with this kind of rotten deal. Having you right there in the palm of her hand, day after day."

Nina's hopes, which had risen slightly, sank again. "I don't think the class can pull anything here in junior high. It's not the same as Experimental. I'd better just go to the office and ask for a transfer to some other class and hope they don't call my parents."

"Dumb! You don't want to do that. It's giving in to the Dark Forces of Evil. Besides, the kids are so excited, it wouldn't be fair to stop them now."

"They didn't lose any time," Nina commented.

"Buzz and the others hate this school so far. It's so cold and impersonal. But now they'll have something to look forward to—giving Mrs. Beckwith the business."

For just a minute, the thought of her father flashed into Nina's mind. The woman was his *wife*. But so what. Here, she was only a teacher. And she didn't belong in *this* school.

"What are the kids going to do?"

"I don't know yet. They're going to work on some plans."

"Don't you have even a hint?" The good feeling was coming back.

"Sure. Miss Big-Talk is already nervous. Why wouldn't she be, having you in class? When the kids get going on her, she'll crack up within the week and go running to the office screaming for a transfer."

Nina let the smile come over her. Of course, that's what would happen. One of them had to transfer out of that class. Better the teacher than her.

 Chapter
4

Nina's big white house looked almost gray in the gloom of the late afternoon. The front steps, she noticed, needed paint even worse than the rest of the house.

It was possible, Nina knew, to get college kids to paint at reduced rates, as they had several summers ago. But her mother had complained last spring, when Nina had mentioned it, that this house was one big money-eating monstrosity. Dad used to do odd jobs around the house, and he still would, Nina bet . . . like putting up the storm windows . . . if only her mother would ask. But that was out of the question.

Even with the tiny lights on in the hall, grayness lurked in the corners. She glanced up the dark stairway and drew back. There were no evil spirits lurking in the corridors above ready to pounce. Still . . .

She was hungry, that was it.

The kitchen, for all its lack of charm, did have a certain warmth. And the soup helped. It really did. She was about ready to reach for the phone when the front door bell went *bur-ring.*

She froze. Mom would come in the back door. Besides, she had a key. Angie had said she had to go shopping. Dad? But wouldn't he call first?

Going down the hall, she wished they had one of those peek-a-boo things in the door like Gram's. The stained glass square was no earthly help.

She took a deep breath and opened the door. Not too wide.

"Hi." A teen-age girl glanced up from a soggy scrap of paper in her hand. "This the Beckwith house?"

"Yes."

"I thought so." She went to the railing of the porch, stuck two fingers between her teeth, and gave a shrill whistle. A beat-up car at the curb screeched off without benefit of muffler.

The girl turned with a laugh. "He's going to total

that heap if he's not careful." Without even looking at Nina, she came to the door and pulled off her sandals. Picking them up by the straps, she said, "I'd have called first but thought I'd better grab the ride."

Although she looked strange, the girl didn't seem particularly dangerous. As she stepped past Nina in the hall, a strange, earthy odor emanated from her leather fringed jacket.

"Which way?"

"Uh . . . down there." Nina pointed toward the kitchen. Although Mom had said not to let anyone in, she couldn't have meant someone who looked as if she might be from the university.

The kitchen light seeped into the hall. The girl followed Nina, still carrying the sandals. Her rough men's pants made a kind of scratchy sound as she walked.

She must have smelled the soup. "Sorry to blast in on you, but I didn't think you'd be eating yet."

"We're not. My mother's not home."

"No kidding. She *is* looking for a girl, though, isn't she? That's what they told me in the employment office."

Suddenly it all fell into place. "Then you really are from the university."

"Right." The girl threw her sandals into a corner. "Who'd you expect?"

"But you're nothing like . . ." Nothing like the

listless creatures they'd had other years, doing as little as they could in exchange for room and board. "I mean . . . I guess Mom forgot to mention she'd put in a call. We've been away."

"I just dragged in today myself. Lucky for me they had a place with a request unfilled."

Lucky for us, too, Nina thought. Not many girls these days were willing to do housework. Linda, last year, had been a last resort and a true drip.

"Big place you have here," the girl said, undoing plastic produce twisters from tiny braids at the sides of her chestnut hair. She raked her fingers through, to get rid of the braids. "How many bedrooms?"

"Uh . . . four."

"How many kids?"

"Just me."

"Wow! Four bedrooms for just the three of you."

Nina pushed the spoon around the puddle of soup in the bowl. "There's just two of us now. Dad, well, he got divorced. And remarried. He lives somewhere else."

"Yeh. Well, there's a lot of that going around these days. What's your name?"

"Nina."

"I'm Merlaine. When did you say your mother would be back?"

"Pretty soon. She works in the city."

"Gee, I don't know then. I'd like to get settled."

42

She pulled the slip of paper from her pants pocket. There was another name beneath theirs.

"How would you like to take a look around?" Nina didn't want this girl—Merlaine—to slip away. They weren't likely to find another at this late date. Certainly none as intriguing. "Our upstairs is neat. We have a turret room."

"Yeh, I noticed when we drove up. Okay."

Again Nina caught a whiff of the jacket as Merlaine moved around, ready to follow.

"It's an old house," Nina explained, leading the way up. "My dad's great-grandfather built it."

"Any ancestral ghosts lurking around?"

Nina clutched the newel post. "Ghosts?"

"Just kidding. Most old families have some ding-a-ling along the line." They reached the top of the stairs. "So that's how a turret room looks. All angles. Don't you ever use it?"

"I used to. For pretend games. When I was a little kid."

"Great place for a seance if we blocked off those windows," Merlaine said, squinting slightly as she took in the high ceilings. "If there's a spook around, this would be the place to flush it out."

Nina couldn't tell whether the girl was putting her on or not. "Some people go for that, I guess." She tried to appear nonchalant. "Do you?"

Merlaine shrugged. "I'm not a nut on the subject

like my aunt Merlaine, but who am I to say? Strange things, strange happenings. I come across them every day."

"Does your aunt believe in spirits?"

"Believe? She's joined the happy crew. Passed over last year."

"Passed . . . ?"

"Died. Croaked." Seeing the look on Nina's face, Merlaine said, "Nothing to get upset about. She was looking forward to it. Said the first thing she intended to do was look up Merlin. You know, the magician from King Arthur?"

Nina blinked. "What does Merlin . . . ?"

"See, my aunt's name was Elaine. Also from King Arthur. But she had this thing about Merlin, so she changed her name to Merlaine. Weird, eh?" She pulled herself away from her slouching position against the doorway and walked to the windows.

"And did your folks name you after her because they were afraid of a curse or something?"

Merlaine rubbed mist away from the window and peered out. "No, honestly, I think my Dad thought some day Aunt Merlaine would leave me a wad of money. Which wasn't the case. She didn't have any." She put her eye close to the window. "Thought that was my friend there for a minute. I told him to give me a half hour."

44

"You've got to see the rest of the house," Nina said, giving her watch a worried glance.

"Okay." Merlaine padded across the floor.

Nina led her across the hall. "That's my parents' . . . my mother's room."

Merlaine made a whistling breath. "I never saw a room with a chaise lounge before. That how you say it? Outside of the movies." Merlaine's look took in everything—the blue-violet tones of the silky rug, the delicate floral bedspread and shimmery curtains, the white and gold furniture. The matching TV.

"It's been redecorated," Nina explained. "Gram did it, long-distance. A birthday present. You can step in if you want to."

"Oh, no," Merlaine said, hands in hip pockets, "I'd better not."

"Here's my room," Nina said, with a wave of the hand, "and yours,"—she ventured—"across the hall."

Merlaine paused at the threshold of the room that had been Linda's last year and walked in, looking around. "All to myself?" Her voice sounded awed. "You mean, all this space just for me?"

For a second, Nina was tempted to show off by saying, "There's an even bigger room down the hall that Dad used to use for his study. It's empty, too." But she didn't. "Haven't you ever had a room to yourself?" she asked instead.

"Never."

"Well, then . . ."

She heard the garage door slam. "Mom's home. Come down and meet her, Merlaine." She grabbed her hand and pulled her toward the stairs.

It wasn't till after dinner that Nina began to breathe easy, pretty certain Merlaine would stay. Hadn't she gone out to the returned car and told the boy to buzz off, she'd see him at registration tomorrow? And hadn't Mom earlier, of her own free will, offered to drive Merlaine back to her friends' house for the night?

"My main concern," Mrs. Beckwith said, twisting the stem of her wine glass, "is to have someone here in the house with Nina. It looks as though I'll be working later and later. Maybe even Saturdays."

"Where do you work, some kind of prehistoric place?" Merlaine asked with her good-natured smile.

"I'm with a perfume company."

Merlaine laughed.

"What's so funny?" Nina wanted to know.

"Couldn't help thinking what a good combination we make," Merlaine said. "I work in a stable, summers."

"Doing what?"

"Grooming horses, exercising them. We live near a resort, see. And this guy runs a riding stable for

46

tourists and summer people. So I help look after the horses."

No wonder her jacket smelled.

"That's a rough job for a girl," Mrs. Beckwith said.

"Not to me. I could live with animals. I'm going to be a vet some day, I hope."

"You mean a lab technician?"

"I mean a vet." She turned to Nina. "How come you don't have any pets running around here?"

Nina glanced at her mother. "They make such a mess. Besides," she added, "I've been away a lot."

"Nina, you haven't told me about your first day at school," her mother said. "How is junior high?"

"Ummmm." It seemed so far away right now. "Okay."

"Did anything interesting happen?"

Nina glanced at the two of them, waiting. This was not the time to go into all that. Besides, if the kids could handle that woman themselves, so much the better. "Mom, you don't do a whole lot the first day." As a smoother-over she added, "I saw the kids from Experimental."

"Experimental?" Merlaine looked interested.

The familiar cramped feeling started coming back to Nina as she remembered how her parents had gone round and round on that one. "You're only taking out your personal hatred of my job by not wanting Nina to go to the campus school," Dad had shouted back one time.

"An apt name," her mother said now, rising from the dinner table. "They used those children as guinea pigs. Trying out educational methods on them." Some of the old lines of irritation appeared on her forehead.

Merlaine stood up. "I'll finish putting the groceries away."

"Let Nina do it," Charlotte said. "I'd like to drive you back to your place before I get out of these clothes."

The two of them had no sooner left when the phone rang. Nina grabbed it.

"Can you talk?" Angie burst out.

"Sure. I'm alone." Nina reached out her foot, pulled over a chair by the rung, and settled down.

"Then get this. The word is out. The kids have a regular telephone marathon going. They've contacted practically everyone. So it's all set for tomorrow."

It took a moment for Nina to tune in to the thought. "What's all set? Oh, you mean with the kids?"

"And you-know-who." Significant pause. "Neen, they're behind you, everyone. Except Rose, of course."

"Behind me in what way? What are they going to do?"

"They're . . . just a minute. Okay, Mom, I'm getting off." Angie's voice lowered. "It's not decided

48

yet, exactly what. A team of experts is working on it. They'll pass the word tomorrow. So be prepared."

"I will, but . . ."

"See you tomorrow."

"Okay. 'Bye." Nina hung up.

Prepared for *what*, exactly?

 Chapter
5

It was weird how, almost twelve hours later (again, just as her mother left for the day) the phone rang. Nina grabbed for it with a welcoming "Hi, Angie!"

"Hello, Nina."

She gulped. "Oh, Dad. Hello. I didn't recognize . . . I mean, I didn't expect . . ."

"Sorry to call so early, Nina, but I wanted to reach you before you left for school." He added, "I intended to call last night, but things got a little hectic around here."

"Your classes haven't started yet, have they?"

"No, but the boys . . . well, anyway . . ." He cleared his throat. "What I'm calling about Nina, is to make plans for seeing you again on Saturdays. How about this week?"

She felt almost scared. It had been so long. He was like a stranger. "I don't know, Dad. We just got back night before last, and we're still not settled . . ."

"I want to see you, Nina." Now his voice was firm, as it used to be.

"All right," she said in a small voice. "Saturday, I guess."

"I'll call Friday about the exact time. We'll find something to do."

"All right, Dad."

"Nina . . . is everything all right?"

What did he mean? Her health? The way she and Mom were getting along? The *woman?* Surely he didn't expect her to leap with joy because she was Nina's teacher. Or did he know?

"Nina?"

"Uh . . . sure." She licked her lips. "Dad . . . I have to leave. The bus." He used to drop Nina off at the campus school . . . before.

"Of course. I'll call back, then, and see you Saturday. Nina, please remember, I love you very much."

She could hardly mumble *good-bye* for the thickness in her throat. She went around the kitchen table, shoving the chairs into place. Why did he have to call this morning and get her all mooshed up? She didn't want to remember her dad just now, with his compassionate eyes and gentle ways. She wanted to blot him out of her memory for the day and concentrate all her thoughts on that teacher and how they were going to fix her. It wasn't easy, but standing with eyes closed, she managed, in a few moments, to summon up the sight of Dolores Beckwith. No, Beck-*witch.* That did it.

Nina left the house, double-checking the front door. She could hardly wait to find out what idea the kids had come up with for math class.

When the Planning Crew told her, during lunch hour, she felt a little let down. "Just that? Is that enough?" She had been thinking in terms of something wild and dramatic, not a little pussy-footing plan.

"Listen, Neen, we've got to ease into this maneuver," Buzz Hendrikson explained, eyes glittering. "Map it all out in a very technical way and cover our tracks so the enemy doesn't zero in on our strategy."

"You sound like some kind of war freak," Cheryl observed. "What did you do all summer, hang out at the movies?"

Buzz glared at her. "You have a better plan?"

"I appreciate what you're doing, all of you," Nina said quickly. "But you really mean all we're supposed to do is just look at her during the whole class without any expression?"

"It's psychology," Ken Bates said, tapping his head. "To throw the poor woman off guard and make her uneasy."

"Sure," Buzz added. "Remember yesterday, we were all pretty responsive, laughing it up." With a look at Nina, he added, "Not knowing the facts. So today, she breezes in, right?"

"With some cheery little remark . . ." Ken said.

"And we all look blank," Angie supplied.

"You've got the idea."

"At first," Buzz said, rubbing his hands together in anticipation, "she'll think maybe we didn't get her little opening gambit. And so she'll bring the humor down to what she thinks is our level. Still no reaction."

"I don't think I could look blank for a whole class period," Cheryl said.

"Now, why do you let yourself wide open with a remark like that?" Buzz asked.

Cheryl's face flamed. "Listen, Bernard . . ."

"Don't fight," Nina pleaded. "Please."

"Or do it some other time," Angie added realistically. "We've got to stick together on this."

Ken agreed. "That's the whole strategy, guys. Every last kid has got to cooperate. Or the thing bombs."

Nina was beginning to see that the plan had

merit. From having lived with a professor father, she knew how satisfying it was to a teacher to have interested students. If during a whole class period the kids showed absolutely no emotion, it would have to leave the teacher thinking *what's wrong with me?*

"You're sure everybody knows about it?" Angie gave a delicious shrug. "This is going to be a riot."

"We made calls last night and finished with contacts today. You guys are the last on the list. We wanted to be sure before we told you." Buzz tilted the folding chair on its back legs and surveyed his little audience in the lunchroom. "There's just one problem. Telephoning's not going to work all the time. Because of some flak from the management."

"His folks squawked about the twenty calls last night," Ken interpreted.

"So the tactical commander will station himself outside the room after class each day from now on to pass along the details of the next salvo."

"Talk English," Cheryl muttered.

"We'll tell you what to do next day, deadhead," Buzz said.

"What's for tomorrow?" Angie wanted to know.

"All in good time, child. All in good time. Just keep your little mind clear for today's session."

The bell rang. They scrambled to their feet, grabbing their trays. Somehow, Cheryl collided with

Buzz's tilted-back chair, which sent him crashing. Her apologies were a little overdone.

"I hope," Angie said to Nina, looking back over her shoulder at the two of them, "that Cheryl doesn't wreck this all up just because of her bitterness."

"What do you mean?"

"You know. How they were madly in love last year until Buzz got interested in electronics and started ignoring her."

"I'd forgotten." Nina wondered if it was worse to be loved and then ignored than never noticed at all.

As the afternoon worked its way toward the eighth period, Nina felt more and more anxious. Would the kids really stick to the plan as a group? Would the teacher suspect? If so, what would she do?

Walking into the room, Nina made a fast check of the kids. They all looked like zombies, except for Rose Hawkins, who wrinkled her nose at Nina as though she had something contagious.

It was almost eerie, the quietness. Here and there a snicker erupted, but it was quickly squelched. The clock's tick sounded amplified.

There was a final settling down as the teacher's heel clicks sounded in the hall.

She bustled in, pink of cheek, as the day before.

"Whew." She made a beeline for the desk and

dropped the load of papers and stuff. "I think I'll have to take up jogging to get in shape for the way they've routed me." She smiled.

Nina, sitting rigidly, couldn't see the faces of most of her classmates from the back of the room, but she could tell from their postures that they were holding to the scheme.

A flicker of surprise crossed the teacher's face. But just for an instant. She smiled again. "Don't worry. I won't collapse on you." Now her look swept briefly across the class as though seeking some glance, some good-natured expression. Her smile slowly faded. For just a split second, Nina felt a twinge. She squelched it.

"Well . . ." Now the woman's voice faked enthusiasm. "Let's dig into some theories and see where we stand."

The class got under way, dully and draggily, as though everyone had been awakened in the middle of the night.

The teacher looked puzzled and then strained. By the end of the period, the glow had been replaced with a *where-have-I-gone-wrong* look.

When the bell rang, the kids dragged from the room as though overcome by boredom. The only bit of action came when Rose, who was edging toward the teacher, got a jolt from behind that sent her hurtling toward the hall.

"I don't think . . ." she began, rubbing her side.

"No one asked you to think. Just follow orders," Scott said. "What's for tomorrow, Buzz?"

Buzz, after glancing into the room, got a few kids into a huddle.

"Tomorrow, to throw her off, we'll act just the opposite. Laugh at everything."

"What if she doesn't say anything funny?" someone asked.

"Then be eager. Act as though math is your one big interest in life."

"That'll take some acting," Marie said. "I hate the stuff."

"Since you're so dumb about it, then," Jeff said ungallantly, "you'd be the perfect stoolie. Ask questions and the rest of us will go crazy volunteering answers."

"Yeah, but be sure your questions are basic things we all know," Buzz said, "or you'll blow the whole program." He gave another glance into the room. "We'd better leave. Pass on the word."

Going home on the bus, Angie made her teeth-together smile. "I never thought I'd ever look forward to math class," she said, shuddering with delight. "But this is like the Fourth of July. You don't know what to expect next."

And it could all blow up right in our faces, Nina thought. She couldn't really believe so many kids could keep a secret. Or keep the plan going until the teacher gave up in despair.

Merlaine was leaning against one of the pillars on the front porch, dozing in the late afternoon sun, when Nina came up the walk. "Hi," she said. "You locked me out."

"Sorry. I didn't expect you back so early. We've got a spare key around somewhere." Her father's. Nina could still picture it lying on the front hall shelf the day he'd left for good.

"Want to help lug up my stuff?" Merlaine asked, rolling down her pants' legs, which she'd turned up to get more tan. "My friends would have, but of course we couldn't get in."

"Sure, I'll help." Nina propped open the door. "Are those boxes full of books?" Her father had almost a truckload.

"Books and bottles, but no booze. Here, you can take the duffle bag. Catch."

Nina sagged slightly under the weight. She looked for the suitcases. There weren't any. "Where are your clothes?"

"You're clutching them, kid. The whole wardrobe. Except for my winter wraparound." She twisted and lifted what appeared to be a horse blanket, rolled up and tied in the middle with twine. "Go on and I'll follow with the delicate things."

Like what, Nina wondered. The electric corn popper had several dents in it already, and that horrible iron desk lamp with the serpent wrapped around its base looked as though it could crack a cement sidewalk.

They made several trips, with Merlaine personally carrying the boxes marked XX. "You can stick around and watch me unpack if you want to," she said, when everything was finally heaped in the room. "I ought to get the bottles out of the way, up on those shelves. Or are you hungry?"

"No, I can wait," Nina said. What was in those precious bottles anyway?

She sat on the end of the bed, which was still stripped down to the mattress, and watched Merlaine open the first box, toss aside crumpled newspapers, and pull out a jar.

What was she expecting? Rock samples? She didn't know. Certainly not anything like that grayish, squishy creature, floating around in some preservative. She put her hand to her mouth.

Merlaine leaned back on her heels and held up the jar to the sunlight. "Isn't he a beaut?" she exclaimed. "I've had Joey here for about three years. Hi, kid." She set the jar down on the floor and pulled out another.

"What . . . is it?" Nina asked, behind her hand.

"Joey? Tadpole. Now I guess you know what this is." She held the second bottle toward Nina.

Nina pulled back slightly and shook her head. It looked like noodles with all the color washed out.

"Round worms. Imagine these in an animal's insides! Doc Lansing gave them to me. Our local vet."

Nina didn't feel like seeing more, but she hated to insult Merlaine, who was eyeing the bottles like treasures. "Why do you have that stuff? I mean those . . ."

"Specimens? 'Cause I'm going to be a vet, like I told you last night." Merlaine started lining up the jars on the built-in shelves. "I tell you it wasn't easy collecting all these goodies. Old Doc finally parted with Sheldon the Snake here, as a combination high school graduation and going-away gift. He's a sweet soul."

Nina wondered if Merlaine meant Doc or the snake. It didn't matter. She could feel her stomach curdle as she watched Merlaine lovingly arrange and rearrange the bottles.

"Joey belongs down front-center since he's the oldest," Merlaine said, switching bottles. She glanced at Nina and laughed. "I'm ragging you a little. I know most people get upchucky about things like this."

Nina straightened. "I don't feel upchucky."

"No?" Merlaine clapped her on the shoulder.

"You're okay. We're soul mates. You know what? I'm starved. Why don't we bring up a snack while I finish unpacking?"

"I'll fix something," Nina said, glad to escape. She paused at the door. "What would you like?"

Merlaine wiped finger marks off a jar. "Something light. Sardines and peanut butter on crackers would be nice. I'm starting a diet."

Nina got a little way down the stairs before she gave out with the gagging sound.

 Chapter
6

Nina wondered that night if she'd ever fall asleep. This quiet was worse than camp. There, with all the commotion, all she'd had to do was pull a pillow around her head to block off the sound (while hoping not to be hit by a hurled object). Here, in her room, there was no way to block off the sights and sounds that flashed through her mind like a TV gone berserk.

She didn't want to think ahead to next Saturday and the things her Dad might say to her. She didn't dare dwell on the things that might go wrong in math class tomorrow. In fact, if she thought about school at all, she'd get so jittery she'd never get to sleep.

She sighed, flopped to her stomach, and cuddled the pillow. She could tell from the bursts of sound that her mother was watching the TV movie from her bed. Nina could go join her, but she didn't want to be reminded of all those nights they'd watched TV after the divorce.

Instead, she decided to pop over to see what Merlaine was doing.

"Oh, it's you," Merlaine said, as Nina scratched at the door. "I thought it might be a mouse, there for a minute."

"Sorry to disappoint you. Are you doing homework?"

"Nope. This is my own book. My boyfriend back home gave it to me for Valentine's Day. Want to see a microscopic study of a goat's gall bladder?"

"No, that's all right." Nina went over and slumped in the chair. Merlaine made herself comfortable in bed again. Nina wondered if she always wore an old shirt and bikini underpants as nightclothes.

After a few moments Merlaine put the book aside. "So what's bugging you?" she asked, clasping her hands around her pulled-up knees.

"How . . . do you mean?"

"However it is. Every time that phone rang tonight you jumped like a grasshopper."

"I'm not jumpy."

"If you don't want to tell me, that's okay." Merlaine reached for the book.

"No . . . wait. Could I sit on the foot of your bed?"

"Plenty of room."

Nina scrambled up and sat cross-legged, facing Merlaine. Creasing the coverlet between forefinger and thumb, she told about the new teacher.

Merlaine gave a low whistle between her teeth. "That's a really rotten deal. What does your mom think about it?"

"I haven't told her."

"Why not?"

"I hate to think of what she'd do. I feel embarrassed enough as it is, without her . . ."

"Can't you tell her, then ask her to lay off? She'd surely understand your feelings, once you explain . . ."

"You just don't know my mother, Merlaine. She never talks about *feelings*. Just about *things*."

Merlaine frowned. "That sounds odd. Boy, you'd better get her to change. And the sooner the better."

Nina thought that over. "How would I begin?"

Merlaine heaved a sigh. "A smart kid like you should be able to figure that out. What's the big deal? Just start talking."

Nina sat thinking, Sure, that's easy enough for you to say.

Wriggling a little, Merlaine scratched her side, along the bikini elastic. "What do you plan to do about the teacher?"

"Cut her down."

"What?"

Nina, switching her thoughts to school, described the plan.

Merlaine looked skeptical. "Aren't you being a little rough on the poor soul? I mean, it's not as though she set the whole thing up, just to make you miserable."

"She could have done something, that first day!" Nina shot out.

Merlaine rearranged her pillow. "Maybe you're right. I guess you guys know what you're doing." After a yawn, she added, "But you'd better hope all the kids cooperate."

"They will. It's a very tight group. We've been together for years and years. Outside kids call us the Experimental Snobs."

"I guess that would make you stick together," Merlaine agreed. "Okay, kid." She settled down under the covers. "Keep me posted."

Nina knew this was her hint to leave, but she still wasn't sleepy. "Did you ever do anything like that in school?"

"Can't say that I did. There were teachers I wasn't wild about, but I was always too busy to let them get to me."

"Busy with what?"

"School newspaper, debate team, acting. I was always in plays. I'm thinking of trying out for the one coming up here at the college. *Blithe Spirit.* Ever hear of it?"

Nina shook her head.

"It's about this couple where the first wife died and the husband remarried and a medium pops around and brings back the spirit of the first wife. I'd like to be the medium. That's the juicy part."

"What's a medium?"

"A person who holds seances and talks with people who've passed over. Something like my Aunt Merlaine."

"Did she hold seances?"

"All the time."

"Could you do it?"

"Probably."

"What really happens?"

"Oh, you ask the spirits for information or to wield their influence. Stuff like that."

The thought of Tom—so unaware of her—flashed through Nina's mind. "Could you hold a seance?" She gave a little laugh. "Just for fun, of course?"

"I might. But give me time. I'll have to work up to the mood."

"How long would that take?"

"As long as it takes to tune into the vibrations of this house. Right now," Merlaine added, "I'd like to tune into some sleep, if you'd be good enough to get off my foot."

The next day at eighth period the ringleaders were waiting at the door. "Shhhhhh . . . she's already in there," Ken warned Nina. "She must be insecure."

"Don't forget," Buzz reminded everyone, "today we really confuse her. We act as though math is the main thing in our lives. We go wild."

Nina lingered after the others had burst into the room. "Buzz, I don't think I can . . ." How could she explain how impossible it was for her to smile and act enthusiastic?

"Oh, Neen, you don't have to," Buzz said, surprising her. "If you did, she'd suspect a plot. She's no dummy. You just sit there and let us take over."

With a grateful nod, Nina went into the room, carefully avoiding even looking at the teacher until she had to.

If the teacher suspected anything, she didn't show it. Her first surprised look turned into a glow of appreciation as some kids outdid themselves asking questions and others practically fell into the aisle, as they wildly waved their hands to give answers.

Once or twice she looked slightly baffled when the very kid who'd asked a simple question later came up with a complex answer to another question. Would she catch on to the conspiracy?

By the end of the class, she was blinking rather rapidly. But she pulled herself together. "I had planned to plunge into chapter eight tomorrow," she said. "I thought you were all ready. But there doesn't seem to be any consistency in your knowledge. I think we ought to take out a day for evaluation. So tomorrow we'll have a little quiz"—she held up a palm against the groans—"just as an inventory. To help you as well as me. It won't go into your grades."

Looking around at the self-satisfied smiles, Nina was reassured. No one was worried. These kids had been tested and retested all during grade school. They lapped it up like milk.

Buzz, who always beat it out to the hall, advised the kids, "Do your best tomorrow. But act bored, as though it's all beneath you."

On the bus, Angie broke up, remembering some of the dumb questions. "I had to drop a book to cover my laugh when Laura came up with that winner about subsets. We had that in fourth grade!" Her laugh erupted like a bubble fountain gone berserk.

"And ten minutes later she knew exactly what a quadratic equation was."

"Yeah." Nina could smile now, but there'd been a bad moment when she thought the whole class would break up. "Don't you suspect *she* caught on?"

"I don't think so." Angie flipped the black banners of her hair over her shoulders. "She's new. And the kids are new to this school. And also, if you want the truth, I think you make her nervous."

"Me?" Nina felt a stirring of pleasure.

"Maybe you don't notice. You always have your head down, staring at the book. But she keeps giving you these glances, as though the one thing she wants in this world is for you to be on her side."

"That'll be the day." Nina tried to frown, but a little smile of satisfaction won out.

 Chapter 7

"Come on over to my house for a while," Angie suggested in the bus, as they approached her stop.

"All right." Nina's mother wasn't home and Merlaine had said she'd be a little late today.

Angie suddenly nudged Nina in the ribs with her elbow. "Look up there at Tom."

Nina hunched her shoulders. She'd never even *hinted* . . .

"That kid sitting with him. Craig," Angie said in a lowered tone. "Isn't he cute?"

"Oh. All I can see is his hair." Blond with springy waves.

"He's new and he's going out for basketball." Angie clutched Nina's arm. "He's getting off with Tom. Coming to our house, I'll bet. I can't stand it!"

The girls followed the group moving to the front of the bus. "See you, Tinsel Teeth," a couple of boys yelled to Tom. Everyone liked him.

He waved nonchalantly.

Angie pulled Nina to a stop to let the boys get a head start. "We wouldn't want Craig to think we're following him."

"It's your house too," Nina pointed out.

The boys were already pulling food from the refrigerator when the girls sauntered into the kitchen.

Angie gave a squeaky little laugh. "You have company."

"Yeah." Tom shoved the milk carton back into the refrigerator.

"Hi," Craig said. He looked directly at Nina. "You Tom's sister?"

Tom glanced around. "Naw, that's Nina."

He might as well have added, "a nobody," Nina thought. Tom wouldn't even want her as a sister.

Angie's laugh was unreal. "No one thinks Tom and I are related. I take after my father. Except for height."

Craig grinned. "Hey, Tom, you must have a good-looking old man."

"Come on, let's take this stuff to my room," Tom said. "Then we'll shoot a few baskets. Angie, Mom wants to see you."

"Did you hear that," Angie hissed, as soon as the boys were out of hearing. "He thinks I'm good-looking!"

"You are," Nina said. Oh, why couldn't she have been born a brunette with definite features? But Craig had thought she resembled Tom. Maybe there was some hope for her.

"Let's get something to eat," Angie said, "or you can, I'm too excited. And then let's go up to my room. We can watch them outside shooting baskets, but they won't be able to see us if we're careful."

"I'm not hungry," Nina said.

"Then let's go. Oh, I'd better see what Mom wants. Mom?" She called out.

"In here, Angela. In the doll room."

Angie made a face. "She's still working on that dumb old wreck she picked up at the auction last week." She ran up the steps to the next split-level and toward the room Mrs. Rafferty had taken for her antique doll collection. "Nina's here, Mom."

"Oh, hello, darling." Mrs. Rafferty made a half gesture, but her hands were occupied with a dangling,

72

wigless doll. "It's been so long since we've seen you. How's everything?"

"Fine." Nina glanced around the room, which was like a toy shop, with antique dolls sitting on shelves, perched in carriages, and even in ancient, miniature high chairs. "You've added to your collection, haven't you?"

"I can't resist new rare ones," Mrs. Rafferty said, "but I sell one of the less unusual types when I can." Her eyes, so like Tom's, settled on a bisque doll with thick, dark curls. "I found her accidentally this summer. She's a genuine Jumeau."

"That's a French maker, isn't it?" Nina asked politely. She'd been in on quite a few conversations with Mrs. Rafferty about dolls.

"Oh, yes. You remember." Mrs. Rafferty gave her own daughter a rueful smile. "I wish Angie took an interest."

"I don't *mind* them." (Angie had told Nina privately that she thought the old dolls looked like a bunch of glassy-eyed goons.) "Did you want something, Mother?"

"I was hoping you'd help steady this head while I try to set the eyes. They keep slipping. But we can do it later."

"Okay, then. Come on, Nina."

Nina was in no particular hurry to hear about

73

how darling Craig was for the next hour. "I'll help," she told Mrs. Rafferty.

Angie didn't mind. "I'll start the research." She put her hand to her eyes, binocular-fashion, to give Nina the idea.

"It's so nice to find a little girl who still likes dolls," Mrs. Rafferty said conversationally, as she showed Nina just how to hold the head.

"Mmmm." She knew Angie's mother didn't mean it as an insult to call her a little girl. "I like dolls all right. Just to look at, of course. Yours, especially. They make me think of olden times."

Mrs. Rafferty, reaching for the tweezers, commented, "I often wish my dolls could talk and tell me about the children who used to own them. I wonder whatever happened to them."

Holding the head, Nina gazed around at the babies in white lace-trimmed dresses and the bigger dolls with ribbons in their long curls. She could imagine little girls of long ago loving and caring for the dolls. They must be very old ladies by now. Like Gram. She couldn't picture Gram as a little girl.

"I think that will do it," Mrs. Rafferty said in a few minutes. "I'll take her now, Nina. Thanks a lot."

"That's okay. Guess I'll go find Angie."

"Yes, I don't want to keep you from your homework. What kind of research is it?" Mrs. Rafferty put the doll on a shelf.

"Mmmmm, it's kind of complicated. Angie's the one who . . . uh . . . knows about it."

Mrs. Rafferty shuffled her fingers through a box of doll parts. "Don't work too hard. And come back soon." She flashed a brief smile. Smiling back, Nina left, wondering, briefly, how Angie and her mother managed to get along so well together. They were so different.

As Nina reached the doorway of Angie's room, she saw her standing in full view at the window, making helpless gestures with her hands.

"They can *see* you," Nina pointed out.

"He wants me to come outside." Angie gave a high-pitched laugh. "Craig. I'm embarrassed."

"You look it," Nina said. Angie never used to act so silly. "Well, go on. I'll leave."

"Oh, no!" Angie rushed over and grabbed Nina's arm. "I can't go out there without you!"

"Why should I go out?" Nina asked, pulling away her arm. *No one wants me,* she thought.

"The boys can teach us how to shoot baskets."

"We know how to shoot baskets." Nina realized she was being obstinate. "We've done it for years in gym."

"Come on," Angie coaxed. "You've got to do it for me. Please?"

Nina had seen that special pleading look of Angie's a hundred times or more, and she knew she was a sucker, but she couldn't turn away. "All right."

"I knew I could count on you."

As they left, Nina asked, "Isn't Tom going out for football this year?"

"He wouldn't dare! Not with all that expensive junk he's got wrapped around his teeth. Let's slow down so Craig won't think we're too eager."

"I'm not," Nina said. "It's your idea, remember. I can't stay very long."

Tom didn't look too happy about the girls joining them, but he didn't look disgusted either. After sinking a couple of baskets, he shot the ball to his sister. She jumped aside with a little squeal. "Catch it, dummy," he said.

"Here . . ." Craig, who had loped after the ball, tossed it gently to Angie.

"Now what?" she asked, raising her dark eyebrows.

"Just stand there and hold it," Tom said. "See if it hatches."

"Ohhh." She bounced it at an angle and Tom swooped, swept it up, dribbled, and sank a slow, graceful basket. He bounced the ball a few times and then suddenly arched to another basket, grabbed the ball as it bounced once, and shot it to Nina. Instinctively, she grabbed it, took a long shot, and made a basket.

"Nice going," Tom said, with a look of surprise. "Go on, keep it up."

She shot and missed, then Tom shot, and suddenly she wasn't self-conscious and flustered anymore as she and Tom set up a rhythm of shooting, hitting or missing, and retrieving the ball.

Angie, she noticed, had given up any pretense of interest in the sport as she blinked her eyes at Craig and kept up a radiant conversation.

Tom was poised for a super-long shot, eyes on the backboard, when three bikes came rattling into the drive and braked near them.

Tom broke his concentration, turned, and with a "Hi, guys," walked toward the three riders, the ball under his arm.

The boys—one of them was Glen something-or-other, Nina remembered—dropped their bikes and started tossing the ball with Tom, who now, of course, pretended Nina wasn't even there. She went to stand a short distance from Angie and then joined her when Craig got into the game.

"How do you like him?" Angie asked.

Nina stalled, blotting her perspiring forehead. Then she realized Angie meant Craig. "I guess he's all right," she said. "I didn't pay that much attention." She wobbled as the ball struck her sharply in the ankles.

"Let's move," Angie said, steadying her. "These guys are rough."

"Sorry, I missed," the kid said, who picked up the ball. He straightened up and gave a half-smile.

"You wounded, Nina?" Angie asked.

"No." She looked curiously at the short, slim boy who had stopped stock-still and was staring at her as though she were a creature from another planet. The boy turned then, and mumbling something, let the ball go, and headed for his bike. He streaked out of the driveway.

"What's wrong with that kid?" Angie looked dumbfounded. "Boy, what a weirdo!"

Angie stared after the boy and then walked toward Tom, with Nina following. "Who was that, anyway?"

"A kid in my gym class. Nichols. What'd you say to him?"

"I didn't say anything! He just took off!"

"He can't help it if he's little."

"I didn't *say* anything," Angie protested. "He just looked at Nina and . . ."

"Oh." Tom's irritated look faded as he, too, looked at Nina. "I guess Roger didn't expect to see you here."

"I don't get it," Nina said.

"You don't?" Tom looked unbelieving. "You don't know who he is?"

"No." Nina stared back at Tom, forgetting that she had always been so shy around him. "Am I supposed to know that kid?"

Tom kept looking for a moment and then took a step backward. "You *should* know," he said. He glanced at the boys and then back at Nina. "He's only the son of that teacher your father married."

 Chapter
8

"I don't see why you're so rattled about it,"
Merlaine said later that evening. Nina was sitting with
her back toward Merlaine's bottled animals. Although
she was used to them by now, she couldn't look at them
while also looking at Merlaine, who was eating pickles
and a peanut butter sandwich in bed. "I mean,"
Merlaine continued, "you were bound to run into that
Roger kid sooner or later."

"But at *Tom*'s!" Nina had told Merlaine about
Angie's brother. "Now I won't feel like going there
again."

"Oh, pooh. I'll bet the kid was more shook up than you. And if he lives clear across town, as you say, he probably won't be back." Merlaine licked some stray pickle juice from her palm and then wiped the spit on the sheet. "Is he in any of your classes at school?"

"No, he's in eighth grade."

"Forget him then. How's your teacher-bugging deal coming along?"

Nina relaxed and smiled.

"We've got her so confused she doesn't even know if she's in the right school." Nina explained the strategy.

Merlaine cleared her throat. "I'm not so sure about you kids."

"What do you mean by that?"

"I mean, maybe you're going a little too far."

Nina pressed her lips together. After a moment she got up. "I'm going to bed."

Merlaine gave a suit-yourself shrug.

At the door, Nina paused. "We're not giving up," she said. "She's going to go. And she can take her kid with her."

Merlaine gave Nina a long look. Then she reached up and switched off the light.

Nina's confidence faded a little as she went from class to class the next day, on the lookout now, in the halls, for Roger. He might pop up out of nowhere, and she didn't want to have to face him.

It was for sure she'd see his mother. Nina wasn't looking forward to eighth hour. The thought of seeing that teacher always rattled her. The test, of course, would be routine.

When the papers were passed out, however, Nina got a jolt. These problems weren't top-of-the-head types. They required concentration. And Nina wasn't prepared for that.

She tried to pull her thoughts together, but she was distracted by the way the teacher drifted up and down the aisle, stopping now and then to clear up a question. When Nina felt the presence behind her, she stiffened, unable to move the pencil. She saw, out of the corner of her eye, the red of the woman's dress as she paused. She seemed to be sending out the message, *Look up at me, Nina.*

Nina wouldn't. She sat stubbornly until, with a touch of her fingers on the desk, the teacher moved forward.

Just keep your distance from me, Nina thought. She worked in a daze, making wild guesses and getting more frustrated by the minute.

It didn't improve her frame of mind to note the smug looks of the rest of the kids as they tossed their tests on the desk at the end of the class. Nina flung hers down and joined the ringleaders in the hall.

"What's for tomorrow?" she burst out at Buzz.

He looked pleased at her down-to-business tone. "We've got a winner. Let's go down the hall a-ways."

Hand on his chin, he eyed each in turn. "Our next tactic calls for complete cooperation. Every guy has got to be briefed."

"I'll make calls," Nina said. "What's the plan?"

"We imitate her," Buzz said.

"Yeah," Ken echoed.

"Every time she touches her hair, about five kids will do the same. If she folds her arms, several kids fold their arms. If she . . ."

"We get the picture," Angie said. "But won't she catch on?"

"Sure, she'll catch on. But what can she do about it?"

"Get mad, for one thing," Lucia Stanfield said.

"So let her get mad," Buzz drawled. "Isn't that right, Nina?"

"That's right. I hope she does get mad. Maybe she'll quit."

"Have we ever made a teach quit before?" Ken asked.

"She's not going to quit," Buzz said. "She probably needs the money. Oops, sorry, Nina."

After a quick glance at her, the others looked away in embarrassment. Buzz continued, "But she's almost got to ask for a transfer after this."

"Yeah, a transfer," Ken said.

"I think you people are terrible."

They turned to see Rose Hawkins at the edge of the group. Whenever Rose got upset, white spots appeared on her cheeks, like frost on a lemon. "Mrs. Beckwith has been very nice to us. Considering." Her look lingered an extra moment on Nina. "It isn't her fault if . . ."

"Shove off," Ken advised.

Rose did.

"I hate to side in with Miss Goody, but she may be right," Cheryl said. "Why don't we take it easy?"

"You can shove off, too," Ken said.

Cheryl didn't.

"Get on with the scheme," Angie said. "We're going to miss our bus."

"What we have to do is assign certain people to imitate her at certain times. Timing is the crucial thing. So our battle plans must be precise."

"General Patton lives!" Cheryl said with a sneer.

"I'll call you, Buzz," Nina said. "And between us, we can contact all the kids tonight."

"Check!"

They rushed to catch their buses.

Nina's mother was especially tired that night. She'd been in conferences most of the day about the new perfume and had even brought work home.

"Shall I take a tray to your room?" Nina offered. It seemed strange. She used to do that in the old days, on Saturdays, when her mother slept late.

"No, I'm going to work in the study on a bridge table."

Good, Nina thought. She didn't want her mother picking up the extension during the school-briefing calls!

"Besides," Mrs. Beckwith said, smoothing Nina's hair from her face, "I'd rather spend a little time with you at dinner. You've hardly told me anything about school. And how about your piano? Have you been brushing up? Don't forget, you have a lesson this Saturday."

"I have to see Dad this Saturday."

"Of course. But what time would that be?"

"He said he'd call Friday . . . tomorrow night."

"Then tell him he'll have to meet you in the afternoon. After your lesson."

Her voice wasn't angry, just weary. Nina bet her mother was sorry now that she had to work. Before the divorce, she did it to show off to Dad's faculty friends. Now they really needed the money.

After dinner, with a sigh, Charlotte headed upstairs.

"I wish she didn't have to work so hard," Nina said, looking after her.

"It takes dough to run a big house like this,"

Merlaine said. "Clear the table and I'll start washing."

As Nina put things into the refrigerator, Merlaine snatched dishes helter-skelter and doused them in the suds. "How's that deal coming along at school?"

Nina described the latest plan.

"Sounds complicated," Merlaine said dryly. "You'd better start calling. Go ahead, I'll finish up."

Nina pulled the phone book out of the drawer.

"Who are you calling first?" Merlaine asked.

"Buzz."

"How come this Buzz character is in charge—I mean, what's his stake in all this?"

"He just likes to run things."

Merlaine didn't reply. Nina got an uncomfortable feeling. It was like the time, when she was about nine, that she had hooked up her sled to a neighbor boy's snow tractor. All she could do was steer a little, but someone else was in control. She dialed. The plan was in motion. It was too late to call a halt.

Buzz, with his battle-plan mind, had charted the seating plan of the math class. He had picked a kid from each row in a zigzag pattern to imitate the teacher for the first ten minutes. He would call those first five kids.

Ken had a list of five kids to call for the next ten minutes. "Old Angie can take the names of the third group," Buzz told Nina. "And Cheryl will call the fourth."

"Cheryl? Are you sure?"

"Sure I'm sure. Her insubordination is just a big act."

Nina brushed off her own annoyance. "I'll take the rest of them," she said.

"I don't know. Maybe you shouldn't get involved."

"I am involved! It's my battle, remember."

"All right, don't get spastic about it. I'll give you the names." After reading them off, he asked, "Are you going to get into the act also?"

"Naturally."

"Suit yourself. But play it cool. Don't overdo it."

Nina nearly reminded him that since this was her battle she'd play it any way she liked. But it didn't make sense to get Buzz riled up. Besides, she had to give him credit. He was taking risks, really big risks, by being the organizer. And he had nothing to gain.

Nothing, she thought, except the natural satisfaction any normal kid would get from rattling a new teacher and driving her up the wall.

 Chapter 9

In grade school, Nina had taken part in a lot of plays.

On this Friday, she had the feeling actors get on the day of performance. A sudden accordion-pleating of the stomach muscles. A dryness of the throat. A preoccupation with time. Six hours from now . . . one hour from now . . .

And now the moment of awfulness.

Going into math class, her heart thumping, Nina sensed that the other kids shared her feeling of stage fright.

The teacher, breezing into the room, paused halfway, like a deer sensing danger. She gave the class a quizzical look before proceeding to her desk.

"Turn to page eighty-seven, please," she said. "We're going to review prime-factorization today."

The only sound in the room was the turning of pages. Almost every head was bent at the same angle over the books. Will they do it? Nina wondered. Will the first group have the courage to begin, or will this stillness also still their actions?

The teacher read the paragraph of explanation and then went to the board and wrote an example. She faced the class, the book held flat against her chest. "Is this clear so far?" she asked.

There was a general murmur of assent. Then Nina saw Dave Reishus in the first row bring his book to his chest. Joyce in the fourth row, farther back, raised her book. Kids in the second, third, and fifth rows followed suit. The teacher didn't seem to notice.

Nina felt her palms perspire.

Mrs. Beckwith read the next paragraph and put the opened book against her again, this time rubbing an itch on the side of her nose.

Almost in unison, the same five kids imitated her. She glanced at them and lowered the book.

The rest of the ten minutes was a fizzle because the teacher was back at the board and there wasn't much to do, copying her.

The second ten minutes she had kids up front working out problems, just to see if they caught on. Two of the kids were from the second group. The remaining three, Ken among them, managed to come up with a few little imitations.

The lesson was going very badly, mostly because everyone was too busy watching the clock and keeping track of their turns to pay much attention to the explanations.

"I don't seem to be getting through to you," the teacher said, shaking her head.

The appointed group dutifully shook their heads the same way.

"Is it because it's Friday?"

She caught Alice Crimpton still shaking her head. "Then what is it, Alice?"

"Uh, uh . . ." Alice gave an unconvincing giggle. "I don't know."

The teacher rubbed her chin. Only two kids dared do the same.

"Let's go over the second paragraph again," the teacher said with a sigh. "That's the vital part, but it isn't all that difficult."

She made some good gestures this time. The kids, flushed with success, openly imitated her, brushing their hands against their hair and then resting them on their throats. A couple of kids, who weren't even supposed to, joined in just for the sport. The teacher seemed to be catching on.

It was the fourth group's turn now. They couldn't do much because the teacher was shooting out questions, standing practically immobile.

Nina's turn was coming up. She felt short of breath.

Now the teacher was back at the board. She finished, turned, and put her hand on her hip. It looked deliberate. Nina's arm felt wooden as she eased it up and rested it on her hip. Buzz, in the next aisle, followed suit. Hesitantly, the three others did the same, with just the sixth one, Grace, either forgetting or chickening out.

There was a flush on the teacher's face. "Let's sum up what we've learned today," she said. The words had a gritty sound. As she talked, she gestured freely. It was too much to keep up with her. Nina would let one go by and then pick up the next. Buzz was practically breaking up. The kids who'd had their turns began to snicker. Rose was getting those white spots on her cheeks.

"Is it clear to everyone?" the teacher finally asked. There was dead silence. "Kenneth?" He nodded. "Melissa, do you understand?"

"I think so."

"Nina?"

Nina stiffened. It was the first time *that woman* had spoken to her directly. She repeated, looking steadily at Nina, "Do you understand what's been going on today?"

It was a direct challenge. Everyone seemed to be holding his or her breath. Nina's look locked with the teacher's.

"Yes," she said, meeting that challenge.

Time seemed to stop.

"All right." The teacher's book made a smacking sound as she dropped it onto the desk. "Do exercises A through K for Monday." Without another word or look at the class, she strode from the room.

For a moment the class hardly moved. Then the bell rang.

"Victory!" Buzz shouted.

That released the tension. With their old Friday cry of freedom, the kids flung themselves into the hall.

"Why didn't you wait for me at your locker?" Angie asked, as she came up to Nina at the bus stop.

"I didn't want to hang around."

"That's right, you're near the office. You don't suppose she reported us, do you?" Angie made her wide-eyed, teeth-together grimace.

"What's to report?" Nina felt wrung out, now that her act was over.

"She caught on, don't kid yourself. But there's

nothing she can do, I guess." Angie relaxed. "Want me to come over?"

"Why?"

"Why? Well, because." She looked dumbfounded. "Don't you want me to?"

"Sure. But I have to get at the piano practice. I have a lesson in the morning." That wasn't really bothering her too much.

"Angie," Nina said, as they boarded the bus, "I have to see Dad tomorrow."

"So is that so terrible?"

"It isn't going to be easy," she said, hoping to make Angie a bit sorry for her. "It'll be the first time in weeks. He may have changed. Especially after what went on this week. I don't know whose side he's on now."

"If he asks any questions, play dumb," Angie advised.

Nina decided to get off at Angie's stop and walk home to put a little space between her and piano practice.

"I wonder," Angie said, just before they parted at the corner, "if the gang will come up with something for Monday. Would you go along with it if they did?"

"Sure. Why not?"

Angie hunched her shoulders. "She's going to let you have it from now on, I'll bet. Did you see that look in her eye?"

"Huh!"

"But don't worry. We'll stick with you. No matter what."

Walking down the street, Nina thought of that slogan, *In union there is strength.* But what happened when you got cut off from the herd? She wasn't looking forward to tomorrow.

Early the next day, her father called to say he'd pick her up after lunch to play tennis. What a relief! She'd rather face him on the courts than across a restaurant table. But she couldn't help thinking, He probably can't afford to take me out to eat anyway. *Oh, Buzz.*

After a painful piano lesson (*We're a little rusty, aren't we, dear?*) and a quick sandwich, Nina sat on the front steps, waiting.

"Under no circumstances are you to invite him into the house," her mother had instructed. "That's not part of the agreement."

Nina swished the racket back and forth across the tops of the bushes bordering the steps. It wasn't a very good racket. Some of the varnish was worn off and the strings weren't all that taut. But she didn't care. She didn't care whether she played well or not. Maybe she'd play punk. Waste a lot of time hitting balls way over his head for him to chase.

Her heart felt as though it had strings pulling it. Tighter than on the racket. *What if he brought that kid along!* That Roger kid, and made them play a game!

But he wouldn't. Her father wouldn't do that.

But what about the other kid, the little one? What if he begged . . . ?

Nina dropped the racket, yanked up her knee socks, and retied her sneakers. Miss Worrisome. Always worrying about what might happen. Dad would just come cruising up alone in the Olds. No, not the Olds. Her mother had that.

Nina didn't recognize her father at first because she hadn't pictured him driving a bright red compact. It wasn't his style. But it isn't his car, she thought, trying not to show her dismay as he got out and came toward her.

Her dad was the same. For a moment, caught in a giant hug, feeling the strength and security of his arms around her, she could only think, It's my dad. Everything's okay.

But in the flurry of kisses, she suddenly remembered where they were. On the sidewalk, in the sun. And with Mother looking out of her upstairs window?

"Let's go," she said, pulling away.

"Nina, I just can't get over it," he said, gripping her above the elbows and looking her over. "The change. In such a short time."

95

"Children are supposed to grow. And change," Nina said. She might as well have added, *Grownups aren't supposed to change.*

She had forgotten how her father had often caught her unspoken thoughts.

He dropped his hands. "So." The joy faded from his face.

"So." Nina repeated. "Where are we going to play?"

He recovered his tone. "I thought over on the high school courts. I checked them out on the way over, and they're practically empty."

"It's a hot day." She started toward the car and halted. Could she really get into that car *she* rode around in?

She slid onto the black vinyl seat, brushed a gum wrapper onto the floor, and rumpled it with her sneaker. She pulled herself in, trying not to touch any more than she had to. Her knees were together, her fingers clutching the racket on her lap.

As they started off, her father's hand looked almost clumsy, working the stick shift. He feels out of place, too, Nina thought. Good.

He wasn't going to ease things for her. She could see that. It was up to her now to start the conversation, after having been so abrupt. She'd already commented about the weather. She raked her teeth over her lips.

How awful to be a stranger to someone you'd loved all your life!

Finally, looking straight ahead, she settled for, "This your car?" Dumb question.

"In a way. It's ours. Dolores's husband was the one who bought it. He died, you know."

"Too bad." There was just a shade of sarcasm in her voice, for which she was immediately sorry. Why do I want to hurt him? she asked herself. *Because he hurt me.*

"Yes, it's a sad thing," her father said, slowing down at an intersection. "Little Paul doesn't even remember his father." He picked up speed. "And there was the little girl they lost. She would have been about eight now. Dolores hasn't had an easy time of it."

Nina said nothing. She knew her father wasn't trying to play on her sympathy. He wasn't the type. But still, she wasn't going to get involved and end up feeling sorry for that woman. She didn't want to think about her.

"We have a college girl staying with us," she said.

"Oh, what's she like? Does cooking confuse her?" He smiled, remembering the blunders of Linda last year.

"Merlaine can cook anything. And eat anything. Last night for a bedtime snack she had turkey noodle soup and grapefruit. The grapefruit part is her diet."

"Is she overweight?"

"Not really. She's just a big girl."

"And the soup part?"

"That's to give her strength, to get her through a night of high-powered dreams. She's a very active dreamer. She writes down the happenings in the morning in case there's a message somewhere. Merlaine's interested in her subconscious. She's interested in a lot of things."

"How about you? Have you tried the turkey noodle method of exploring your subconscious?"

"To tell you the truth, no. I don't care much for noodles. Not since the round worms."

Her father practically braked the car. "You have worms, Nina?"

"Nope. But Merlaine does. In jars." She told her father about Joey and the other specimens. "They almost made me upchuck at first," she admitted. "But now they don't bother me a bit. Things aren't bad once you make up your mind to face them."

"That's right, Nina," he said, pulling into the parking lot.

Oh, boy! Why had she made such a dumb statement? She had let herself wide open for a heart-to-heart talk.

 Chapter
10

She knew the time had come for the talk after they'd finished playing and were sitting on a bench eating ice-cream bars.

"I understand, Nina," he said, "that your math class isn't all it should be."

"Mmmmmmm?" She pulled off a section of chocolate and popped it into her mouth.

"Would you care to tell me about it?"

Nina made a great show of licking the stick where the ice cream was dripping. "Tell you about what?"

"Let's not play games."

With a kid, Nina would have said, "We just played a game. Tennis." With her father . . . well, you just didn't get that cute. But she wasn't about to say anything until she knew how much he knew. She settled for, "It's the same kids who were in my math class last year."

"Accelerated, right?"

"Yeah. That's right."

"So they should pretty well know the subject."

"What subject?"

"Math, Nina. Math." He crumpled the paper around his stick and rose to toss it into a trash basket.

"You know, I know, and the teacher knows that these students are capable of doing superior work." He paused. "They're also capable, it seems, of rising to great heights of loyalty, or depths, as the case may be."

"I don't know what you're talking about." She did, actually, but her mother had often said, "George, cut the professor talk around the house, why don't you, and speak plain English."

He seemed to remember, too. "I'll put it bluntly, Nina. Those students are deliberately acting up. I suspect because of you."

"Me?" She broke her now-empty stick in half and tossed it toward the basket. It caught on the rim. "Why are you blaming me?"

"I'm not blaming you. Believe me, Nina, I understand. And I sympathize. Just as your friends sympathize. But they're not helping you. Not really."

"You're on her side."

He ran his hands through his hair and leaned back. "It's not a question of taking sides. It's a question of making the best of a situation."

Angry tears sprang to Nina's eyes. She picked up her racket and poked her fingers through the holes.

"It's tough. Very tough," her dad continued. "I realize that. As she does. But it's her job to teach the class. And control it. One way or another."

Nina concentrated on her fingers.

"She was assigned to these students because of her special teaching abilities. She has a lot to offer, Nina, and in the long run you'll benefit. As soon as you learn to transcend . . ."

"Do what?"

"Transcend. Rise above it. Try to rise above the fact that she's—"

"Your wife."

"My wife. Yes." He seemed almost relieved to say it.

Nina's fingertips were turning pink and puffing a little. Angrily, she pulled them out of the squares. "I don't see why I should have to suffer," she said, "just because . . . because . . ."

"Because what, Nina?"

"Because you two got a divorce. You and mother."

Leaning forward, elbows on knees, Nina's father was silent a few moments. Then he said, "We thought our fights were destructive to you, Nina. The look on your face—especially that awful time we argued about selling the house—I'll never forget it."

"I don't care how I looked. At least you two were together."

"In the same house. But not together." He raised up and put his hand on the bench in back of Nina. "Honey, we tried. For your sake. But when differences are that great, the resentments run deep. No child should be raised in such a hostile atmosphere. We've separated, yes. But you still have Mother. And you still have me."

Nina trembled, but she said it. "And you have Dolores."

"Yes, I have Dolores. Life has some rewards."

Boy! "And what about Mother?" Nina blurted. "Mother has to work now."

"Nina, be fair. Your mother chose to work before . . . before all this happened."

"Because you two didn't get along."

"That's what I've been trying to tell you, Nina. She didn't like my way of life. She didn't like my profession, my colleagues—and finally, me."

Nina ground her heels in the dirt. "So now what am I supposed to do about it?"

"Try to understand. Face things as they are. Cooperate a little."

"How? By letting *her* boss me around in school?"

"I can't believe Dolores is bossing you around, as you put it. Can you honestly say that?"

Nina bit the inside of her check. "I don't want her for a teacher."

Her father rubbed a hand across his forehead and then rose from the bench. "All right, Nina. Maybe it is asking too much. What shall I do? Call the school and ask to have you transferred to another class? Or shall I call your mother and let her handle it?"

She didn't answer.

"Well, Nina, what do you want?"

She swallowed. "I'd like to think about it."

"Whatever you say."

Why, she thought, walking beside him, couldn't he be a mean father? It was awfully hard to stay angry with someone who was trying so hard to find a happy way out.

But why couldn't he have found a way to make happiness come at home?

 Chapter
11

"What did you and your father talk about all afternoon?" her mother asked at dinner that night.

"We played tennis."

"And?"

Nina just looked at her mother.

"Surely, you talked about *something*. Wipe that milk off your mouth, please."

Nina did. "Sure, we talked."

"Well?"

This wasn't fair. "We talked about school and stuff."

"That figures." After a pause her mother asked, "And how are things going at . . . home?"

"He didn't even mention it. Mom, I'd rather not talk about Dad. Okay?" She gave Merlaine a sideways glance that was supposed to say, *See? She doesn't talk. Just asks questions.*

Merlaine jumped up to answer the phone. It was for her.

Mrs. Beckwith excused herself, saying she was cutting out desserts. Nina ate her pudding without tasting it.

She started clearing the dishes, but Merlaine, talking away like crazy, motioned her to leave.

Okay, then, let her do the work.

Going upstairs, Nina felt distinctly unwanted.

No, that wasn't true. She looked at the closed door to her mother's room. Mom tried to talk. It wasn't her fault if she didn't have Dad's easy way. Here she'd been all alone in the house all summer, not once complaining about Nina's being at camp. And now that I'm home, Nina thought, I just ignore her.

She decided to do something about it. She'd spend the evening with her mother doing girl stuff and watching TV, the way they'd done for comfort during those months of the divorce.

After digging around in her junk drawer, Nina found the manicure kit Gram had sent several birthdays ago. Then she knocked on her mother's door.

"Who is it?"

Who is it? Who did she think it was? "Me, Mother. Can't I come in?"

"Of course."

Nina stopped at the threshold, amazed. "Mother, you've got your face on!" Then she eyed the new dress her mother was taking from a hanger. "Where are you going?"

"Just out with Phil."

"Phil?" *The voice on the phone that night.*

"I told you about him."

"You did not."

"Oh." Charlotte struggled with the zipper. Nina stood there and let her struggle. "Phil is someone I've been seeing off and on. Very pleasant. You'll like him."

"You didn't *tell* me you were going out."

"All right, Nina, I'm sorry. He just called this afternoon, and what with one thing and another . . ." She picked up the hairbrush and smoothed a few stray wisps. "I'll be home fairly early. And Merlaine won't be out long."

"Merlaine? Her too? Where is she going?"

"To a campus movie with some boy." Charlotte saw Nina's look in the mirror and turned. "Well, it is Saturday night, love. The girl has a right to some social life."

And what about me? Nina thought. Don't I

count? It didn't seem right, watching her mother get ready to go out with some man other than Dad. It just didn't.

"There's the doorbell," Charlotte said. "Come on, come down and meet my date."

Nina followed, grumbling. Still, she didn't mind checking him out.

A moment later, shaking hands with Phil, she decided he looked like some guy from a station-break commercial.

"You're a tall girl," he said, smiling the way the guy did, when forty seconds after taking a pill, he was free of minor aches and pains. "How old are you?"

"Twelve."

"Nina's quite athletic," her mother said, probably to excuse her crummy appearance. "She's been playing tennis this afternoon."

"With my father," Nina added.

"Oh. That's nice." Phil looked as though he could stand another pill. "Are you ready, Charlotte?"

Alone, Nina got out a macramé wall hanging she'd started at camp and began knotting.

The real knot was in her stomach. She didn't like the way things were going at all.

Mom wasn't nearly as helpless (or as lonely!) as Nina had imagined. Merlaine had a life of her own. Dad certainly had a life of his own. And so who was left for Nina? Her friends.

She didn't want to be cut off from them to make her way alone in that new school. And so it followed that she didn't want to be transferred out of Accelerated Math. Together—even with *her*—was better than being alone.

On Monday, as their group was leaving the lunchroom, Nina told Buzz she had decided to call off the campaign.

Buzz was flabbergasted. "What do you mean?" he burst out. "*You've* decided!"

"It's the best thing," Nina said nervously. "If we go on, all we'll do is get into trouble."

"Trouble is my middle name."

"Your parents have weird ideas," Cheryl said. "Now, *my* middle name . . ."

"Stash the humor," Buzz said. "Listen, Nina, don't think we're going to quit now, just because of a little flak. No one said you had to do battle. But just don't interfere, okay? Remember, I'm in command."

"You're not in command! You have the idea you're some kind of super-genius!"

Buzz looked at Ken for support. "Get this kid. When the fighting gets rough, she says, 'Oh, stop! I don't want to play any more!' "

"Shut up!" Nina hit his upper arm with a book.

"Let's leave," Buzz said to Ken. "These kids make

me sick." He waited until he got down the hall before he rubbed the sore spot.

From the looks of the ringleaders in math class, Nina knew they were going ahead with the plan. Whatever it was.

And from the determined look on the teacher's face as she strode into the room, the plan would not go unchallenged.

Mrs. Beckwith's eyes weren't sparkling today. They were shooting out warning signals. Don't they *notice?* Nina wondered, as the students, following the brisk order, got out their homework.

Taking up her book, the teacher said, "Beth, please read the first problem aloud. Then tell us how you went about solving it."

Beth dutifully obeyed orders.

"Good. Next problem, Rosemary."

"Oh, Mrs. Beckwith," Rosemary said in a put-on voice, "I forgot my math book."

This was it. Nina felt a prickle at the back of her neck. She glanced at the backs of the other pupils. She knew them well enough to know something was astir.

Two problems later, Ken said, "I forgot my math book." His voice had a false bravado.

The teacher just looked at him. He snatched Cheryl's book from across the aisle and read the problem.

·Nina noticed the teacher taking quick inventory of the desks. By squirming, Nina saw that at least twelve kids had no books. The sure-of-themselves kids.

Now the teacher pounced. "Buzz! Next problem."

"Gee, I'm sorry. I don't have my . . ."

"All of you people"—the teacher's voice was low and cold as a glacier—"who *forgot* their books can just toddle down to the office. And be sure you show up with a permission slip tomorrow. If you decide to come back."

"Hey!" Buzz mustered huge outrage. "Just for . . ."

"Just leave," the teacher said, staring him down. "Goof-off time is over."

As though from far off, Nina heard the undertones of grumbling and phony innocence as the kids shuffled toward the door. Without realizing what she was doing, Nina arose and gathered up her books.

She reached the front of the room.

"Nina!"

She turned.

"Do you have your math book?"

Nina was drenched in shame and sweat. "Yes, but . . ."

"Then sit down, please."

"But . . ."

"Would you please take your seat?"

Nina hesitated between the angry scowl of Buzz

as he turned at the door and the cold command of the teacher.

Drooping, she returned to her seat.

She was like a robot, programmed to respond, during the rest of the class. At the close, the teacher had somehow maneuvered to the back of the class.

"Nina, I'd like to see you for a few minutes," she said, just before the bell rang.

Nina stayed.

Angie hovered near the door after everyone else had left.

"Angela, please run along," the teacher said. She waited until Angie disappeared from sight and then sat on the desk diagonally in front of Nina. Nina's fingers left damp smudges on the books she straightened on the seat beside her.

There was a pause. Nina waited, eyes on the desk top. The varnish had streaked in one place.

"My dear, I'm sorry."

Nina took a quick little breath. She hadn't been prepared for this. The voice so soft and full of concern. Almost like a mother's . . . no! She tightened her will.

"I blame myself," the woman said. "I should have made it my business to check the pupil list before school started. But I had so many other things—" She stopped.

Nina, hunched, wiggled her shoulders slightly.

"Even after that first day, when I realized . . ."

She cleared her throat. "I guess I'm an eternal optimist. I thought we could work it out."

Nina lifted her eyes as far as the woman's interlaced fingers. The wedding band was plain and very narrow.

"And I didn't dream things would get so out of control."

Finally, Nina choked out, "It was my idea."

The teacher half laughed. "I don't imagine it took much convincing. Not with this group."

"We've always been together," Nina said grudgingly.

"I realize that. It's a great bunch of kids. Fine minds. But that mental power could be put to more profitable use."

Nina made the nervous gesture of teeth raked over lips. "I'll get transferred. Like my dad said."

In the quiet, she finally looked right at the woman.

"If that's what you really want, Nina, of course. If you find me so"—she hesitated—"unbearable."

Nina hated herself. Her eyes were actually misting.

"But I had hoped we could come to some working agreement. Declare a truce." The woman smoothed her skirt. "I hope you'll believe me when I say I realize what you're enduring. I don't ask you to accept me out of class. If some day you do, I'll be . . ." She swallowed and looked away. Fleetingly, Nina thought of the little girl who would have been eight years—forget it!

"I'll be . . . grateful." The woman had regained control of her voice. "But what we're facing is *now*. This class. Tomorrow and tomorrow and tomorrow. Can we do it, Nina? Can we forget who we are and regard each other simply as teacher and student?"

Nina would miss her bus. She would sit there forever, in silence, with that woman. Waiting.

She couldn't talk. Finally, with teeth firmly clamped over her lower lip, she nodded her head.

The woman stood up.

Nina tightened. *If she lays a hand on my shoulder, if she presses her advantage and . . .*

She didn't.

"Thank you, Nina. It's all I could ask." Her voice became almost whispery. "I'll make it as easy for you as I possibly can." She took a few steps to the front and turned, now with a smile. "Without singling you out for special privileges."

Nina found it possible to return a sort-of smile.

She gathered her books and started for the door. She had to stop. She swallowed. "What about the others? They did it because of me."

Mrs. Beckwith started putting stuff into her briefcase. "Don't worry. A brisk official warning won't break their spirits. They'll be back tomorrow with some of the starch out of them. That's all. Then maybe we can get down to the business of math."

For just a second Nina felt a force—like an electronic ray—pulling her toward this pleasant woman. She fought it off.

"I'll miss my bus," she said flatly.

She dashed down the hall and outside and waved to the driver, who was revving up the engine.

Angie shoved over to make room on the seat. "Well?" she asked, face full of anticipation.

"I . . . I told her off."

"Good!"

Nina sat with arms folded against her chest, staring straight ahead. She took satisfaction in the awed, unnatural silence of Angie.

Blocks later, when Angie tapped her shoulder, Nina swung sideways toward the aisle to let her off at her stop. She watched Angie get off.

Just before the bus started up, their looks met through the open window. Nina leaned out and yelled, "I really didn't!"

"I know!" Angie yelled back.

 Chapter
12

That night, Angie made a few calls. On the bus the next morning, she gave Nina the full scoop of what had happened in the office.

"They didn't even get a detention," Angie reported. "Of course, Buzz tried to take the whole blame—you know him, 'Never mind the blindfold, I'll face the firing squad!' What a show-off!"

"Go on!"

"Oh, then everyone chimed in, wanting their share of the glory. You know how they are. They didn't even mention you."

What a letdown. "And then what?"

"The principal sounded off a while about junior high being the training ground for high school and how it was time to shape up, et cetera. Then he let them go."

"What do you think will happen now?"

"It all depends," Angie said. "If she's the kind to hold a grudge . . ."

"She isn't," Nina said. "I meant the kids."

"They just feel it was fun while it lasted. Now they'll turn their feeble little minds to something else."

Nina was right about the teacher. All she said to the class was, "If you're through fooling around now, let's get down to math." And the kids, as Angie predicted, were good-natured about being found out. No one even gave Nina a disgusted look.

Starting fresh, the teacher explained a new concept. The kids grabbed onto it and began racing away at their own speeds, just as they'd always done in Accelerated.

For Nina, working individually was murder because it meant she had to discuss her assignments directly with the teacher. She stalled for two days, pretending she was a slow worker. But pride finally forced her to show her work. Mrs. Beckwith didn't make any big deal of it. Nina could have been just any pupil.

By Friday, math seemed just like any other class.

But after school that day, Nina remembered the bad times weren't over. Tomorrow, she'd see Dad. He was sure to want to clarify everything. He always did.

For a while she was almost fooled into believing this time he would let the matter drop. They were visiting a new nature preserve, walking in the silence along shady paths, pausing now and then to read a marker that told about the type or age of a tree or about the prairie grasses.

They stopped to listen to scurryings in the leaves beyond the path. "This reminds me of *Wind in the Willows*," Nina said. "I wish we could see some animals."

"Let's come back when there's been a light snow. At least we can see the footprints."

"Pawprints."

"Speaking of paws . . . shall we? Pause?"

"Oh, Dad!" She scuffled with him and landed, laughing, on his lap, at a resting bench.

"Nina." He held her close, and suddenly they sobered. "I'm so glad to see you like this again."

She stiffened ever so slightly.

"Are you feeling better now . . . about every-thing?"

She slid out of his arms to the bench beside him. "I guess so."

"And have you thought about . . . about what you want to do?"

"I guess I'll stay in the class."

"I'm glad, Nina. And I must say I'm gratified that your mother went along with it."

She didn't dare look at him. "Did you call Mother?"

"Naturally not. Past experience has shown—well, you know. Anyway, it's better that you explained it to her from your point of view." He got up, and so did Nina.

She was thinking of admitting that she *hadn't* explained it to her mother when he continued.

"And as for Dolores, she's really excited about your class. Every night at the dinner table, she has something new to say about some kid or other. I almost believe Roger wishes he were in there with all of you."

In an off-handed way, Nina remarked, "I met Roger the other day. After school."

"So I heard."

She shot a quick glance at him. "Does he tell you *everything?*"

"I doubt that. But he mentioned he was at the Raffertys', and I said you were a friend of Angie's. Then he said you were there, too."

"How did he know who I was?"

"I didn't ask. I assumed someone told him. Or maybe he recognized you from the pictures on my desk."

Her pictures! How strange, in another house. She

didn't know whether she liked that or not. "Do you talk about me?"

"Sometimes. Little Paul is quite fascinated by the subject."

"Why is he fascinated by me?"

"He can't understand why 'Daddy's big girl,' as he calls you, doesn't live with us."

(Daddy! You're not his daddy!) "He sounds dumb," she said.

"Oh, Nina, he's only three. Not much more than a baby."

"If he's so little, who takes care of him when . . . ?"

"When his mother's teaching? A neighbor. She has a boy the same age. Do you want to turn back? This path seems to wander for miles around that pond."

"Okay. I'm getting hungry."

At seven o'clock, full of pizza and full of courage after being with her father, she walked up the stairs. This was the time to tell her mother about Dolores-the-teacher, Nina decided. If she said it all in a rush—now —her mother would have time to cool off before Monday. At any rate, Nina told herself, there's nothing Mother could do. Not if I want to stay in that class and both Dad and the school back me up.

She was halfway up the stairs when she heard her

name mentioned in her mother's room. Who? Oh . . .
it was only Charlotte on the phone.

". . . will be with her father, I assume. Anyway,
isn't it a bit early to be talking about Christmas?"

Nina knew she shouldn't listen, but she couldn't
resist.

"Mother, I'm not going to talk to him about it.
George only calls me when it's absolutely necessary,
and I wouldn't call him unless my life depended on it."

There was a short pause. Nina heard the click of
her mother's cigarette lighter. "Well, I'm sorry," she
said then. "I don't mean to be irritable, but I have
things on my mind. What?" Another pause. "No,
Mother, nothing so dramatic. It's just that my job is a
killer. I'm worn out by the weekend."

Nina drifted to the doorway.

"Oh, yes, the college girl's a help, but even so,
with this barn of a house! I'd like to sell it and move to
the city." She caught sight of Nina. "Here's your
granddaughter now . . . just a second."

Nina took the phone, still warm from her mother's
hand. "Hi, Gram." (Did Mom really mean all that?)

"And how's my precious?"

"Just fine." (Move to the city!) "I've been out to
the nature center."

"How nice. I just returned from a concert."

"Was it good?" She almost said a *good group*.

"Simply elegant. You know how they dress at benefits. Oh, and speaking of clothes . . ."

Nina vaguely listened as Gram talked about Saks and so forth and then tuned in again to " . . . so busy, but I promise I'll pop over next week."

"Pop over?" Nina asked, confused. "Here?"

"To Saks, dear. For your clothes. Can't you hear?"

"I can now."

Gram cleared her throat. "Tell me, how is . . . everybody?"

Nina knew what she meant, but she wasn't going to say one word about Dad. "Fine."

"Oh. Well, that's wonderful. Now, darling, write to me. And put your mother back on, will you?"

Nina left for her room, but on the way she heard her mother comment, "I don't know. Nina has never mentioned her."

For a moment, Nina felt almost guilty, as though it was wrong for her to have any connection with Dad's new wife. But what was wrong with it, she'd like to know?

As she changed her clothes, the old anger arose against Gram. Why did she always have to butt into their lives with her cracks about Dad and the house and everything? All she did was get Mom all stirred up and put ideas. . .

"Did you have a good time this afternoon?"

Nina looked warily at her mother, strolling into the room. "Yeah. It was okay."

"Where did you go?"

"You heard. To the nature center."

"The last of the big spenders, eh?" Charlotte absently straightened things on Nina's dresser. "Did you have dinner?"

"Yes." She thought, Why don't you just come out and say what you're thinking, instead of hitting me with all these questions?

"You had dinner just with your father?"

"Yes."

Her mother started to leave. "So you didn't see—that woman?"

"Today, you mean? No. It was just me and Dad."

"Dad and *I*." Charlotte left then, with Nina deciding this was not the time to spring the Dolores story.

During her bath, Nina brooded about that house thing she'd overheard. Was Mother really fed up with the place or had she just said so to make Gram feel good? On her one visit, Gram had declared the house impossible and had cut short her stay. But then she considered any place primitive that didn't have a doorman and maid service.

In nightgown and robe, Nina went across to her

mother's room. "Aren't you going out tonight?" she asked.

"I'm not going stead-y," her mother replied in a schoolgirl voice, and laughed.

"Merlaine goes steady. Only not with the same guy. She just goes."

"She doesn't have a daughter to keep her company. Come on, love, and watch TV with me. And let me brush your hair. Tsk, such a pony!"

Nina hesitated, remembering Merlaine's advice about talking things out. But surely, this wasn't the time. Why spoil her mother's present carefree mood?

Obediently, Nina sat at the foot of the chaise, unmoving as her hair was brushed, combed, and lifted this way and that. I feel like one of Mrs. Rafferty's dolls, she thought. Mommy's little toy, for her to fuss over, to cuddle, and then to tuck away nice and neatly. But, she resolved, one of these days she'll find out I'm not her little doll any longer. I'm going to make her start treating me like a real girl, a girl who's growing up and who deserves some answers.

Some time soon. Some time soon they'd have to start telling and *trusting*.

But not tonight.

# Chapter
13

The box from Saks was leaning against the front door one afternoon a couple of weeks later when Angie came home from school with Nina.

"It's addressed to you! What is it?" Angie asked.

"Oh, clothes."

"Oh, clothes," Angie mimicked. "You're so blasé." She obligingly lugged the package upstairs and, with the scissors Nina handed her, started cutting the twine. "Maybe there's something cool to wear to the dance."

"Huh!" Then it sank in. "What dance is that?" Nina asked.

"At school. Where else? Tom's on the committee. All the student council kids are, to his disgust. Wow, would you look at this!" Angie held up a plaid dress with matching jacket. "And there's more. Neen, you ought to be doing this."

"Go ahead," Nina said. "I didn't ask for it."

"Two skirts, three sweaters, and ohhhhhh!" Angie pulled away tissue and held up a blue velveteen dress edged at the neck with lace. "It's gorgeous. But why would she send this kind of dress?"

"That's my Gram. Don't you dare tell anyone."

"I won't." Angie smoothed the back of her hand along the lush fabric. "She must be living in the past, your grandmother."

"She sure is." There was a photo, somewhere, of Charlotte at the age of eight in just such a dress. Only she looked " . . . like a princess," Gram had said. "Sitting there with those beautiful curls and those enormous blue eyes, the color of her dress." And wearing white gloves and sitting with ankles properly crossed, waiting for a little gentleman to ask her to dance.

Angie folded the clothes back into the box. "What will you wear to the dance?"

"How should I know? Hey, there's Merlaine!"

Nina could tell by the way she banged the door and clattered up the stairs. "You're late!" she yelled, partly to show off.

"Had to meet with the costume chairman. Who knows zilch. Hi, Angie."

"She's in *Blithe Spirit*," Nina explained. "A play about uh . . . spirits."

Without invitation, they followed Merlaine to her room. "Only Merlaine's not a spook," Nina added. "She's the medium."

"Yeah, I go into trances," Merlaine said, flinging her fringed jacket onto the bed, "and bring back people who've passed over."

Nina and Angie exchanged glances.

"I already told Angie we might have a seance here some night," Nina said.

"It'll have to be after the play." Merlaine, who had been scooting garments back and forth in her closet, sighed. "Nothing here. I knew I should have brought some of Aunt Merlaine's trappings along. Now I'll have to run home one of these weekends to get them."

Angie looked baffled. Nina explained, "Her aunt was some kind of . . ."

"Nut," Merlaine supplied.

Angie's glance flicked to the jars, as though to indicate Merlaine wasn't all that average.

"Her aunt was really some kind of mystic," Nina said. "Isn't that what you'd call her, Merlaine?"

"I guess so. She kept to herself, grew herbs, mumbled under her breath a lot. Except for me, hardly anyone went near her in the last few years. She did have some strange habits. One of which was not taking baths."

"Why was that?"

"She had built up this aura . . ."

"I'll just bet," Angie said, holding her nose.

Merlaine gave her a playful shove. "Much more of that, pre-creep, and you won't come to the seance."

Word got around the school quickly about the dance even though there was as yet no official notice. Finally, on Friday morning Miss Primrose announced it would be held the following Friday night from seven until nine-thirty. "It's not a date affair, and dress will be casual," she said. "Not too casual. No skimpy outfits, please." Her look carefully avoided a girl who'd been sent home because of bare skin showing around the midriff. "I'm sure there'll be notices, but keep the date in mind."

After class, Angie asked Nina if she wanted to stay and help make posters. "Tom's in charge and conned me into helping. He can't letter at all. Come on, Nina."

"How would I get home?"

"There's a late bus Fridays. Because of kids on detention."

"All right, I'll stay if you really need me." (If Tom needs me.)

"We're supposed to go to the gym. They'll have supplies."

Nina wondered why they needed so much help with about twenty kids on the school council. She saw why when she and Angie reached the gym.

There were tables, long rolls of paper, and marking pens but only three workers. One boy and two girls.

"Some of the kids had to go to chorus," an eighth grade girl explained. "And those guys"—she glanced at the boys shooting baskets—"they're lost causes when it comes to art."

Tom saw his sister and, after tossing the ball to someone, jogged over. "Thought you weren't going to show up. Here's the one I'm supposed to do."

"Nina's going to help."

For once, he looked right at her. "Hey, you're all right."

Nina nearly died.

"Boy," Angie grumbled, "you're going to have to dance with us for doing all your work."

"Why would you want to dance with me?"

"I wouldn't *want* to," Angie said. "Except to get started and give other people the idea. Isn't that right, Nina?"

How could she do this! Even though Angie didn't *know*, she shouldn't just . . .

Nina was saved from answering by the yell of some kid from the floor, "Hey, Metal Mouth, what are you doing over there?"

"Giving orders." Tom laughed and dashed back to the others.

"Why did you have to say that?" Nina hissed. "About dancing with me—I mean us."

"Don't worry," Angie said. "He won't bother you. Tom's Mr. Clumsy except when it comes to sports. A real klutz."

The eighth-grade girl, who had taken in the conversation, now said with contempt, "Don't you know that no one actually dances at these things?"

Angie stared. "Then what do you do?"

"You stand around and drink cokes and talk to your friends."

"Then why make posters?"

The girl gave the amused boy at the table an I-don't-believe-this look. Then, spacing her words as though talking to a backward child, she said, "We make posters so people will know to come to the *dance*."

"You don't say." Angie motioned to Nina, and

they began blocking out and filling in the letters. Every once in a while a basketball bounced against their legs or jiggled the table.

Angie got slammed a couple of times and complained to Tom. "It's bad enough, doing this boring thing without getting batted around. Besides, even you should be able to help fill in these letters. It doesn't take any talent."

"Okay, it's getting late." But Tom went over to help the boy, not them.

"I'll help." Another boy took the felt marker. Nina glanced and then glanced again. The feeling was like cold water against her chest. It was *that kid.* That Roger.

He had the same reaction. Shock. Suddenly Nina felt sorry for him.

"Start there . . . why don't you?" she said, pointing.

Like a little kid on the first day of school, following orders, Roger ducked his head and began filling in the wording.

They worked away silently. Nina was catching up to him. "You don't have to be so careful," she said, trying to sound natural. "It's only a poster."

He nodded and speeded up.

Nina was trying so hard to keep from thinking about who this boy really was, she didn't notice anyone standing behind her. Then Tom's voice said, "Move over, I'll do this part. We've got to get out of here, the janitors say."

Nina looked up and gasped, "Where is everyone?"

"They scrammed to catch the bus."

"How about us!"

"You've missed it." Tom laughed at her look of panic. "But you've got a ride. Rog's mom will drop us all off."

"You jerk!" Angie spat out. "You could have asked!"

"Well, why . . ." Then Tom realized. An embarrassed flush spread over his face.

"Tom . . . she won't mind. My mother," Roger said to his hero. He looked toward Nina for help.

"It's okay with me if it's okay with her," Nina said. Oh, boy, that was a jolt.

As they were hurrying toward the door, Mrs. Beckwith looked in. "I was wondering if you people were finished," she said. "They're jangling keys in front of my face."

Tom explained about the bus. "I could call home, though, and see if Dad's there."

"Don't be silly. It's no bother. And you all live in the same direction."

They went to the familiar red car in the parking lot.

"Why don't you girls sit in front with me?" Mrs.

Beckwith said easily. "Nina, if you sit next to the door, I'll drop you off first and work back."

She did know where Nina lived. Of course. And she was making it easy for her. How awful it could have been if she'd dropped the others off first, leaving Nina in the car with her and Roger!

Weaving through the thickening traffic, Mrs. Beckwith asked if they had seen a recent TV documentary about UFOs and what their theories were on sightings. Tom said he thought it was a lot of guff and he wouldn't believe in UFOs until he saw one. Angie countered with "proofs" she'd read in a recent best seller.

"My father says . . ." Nina caught herself. How could she have forgotten! "He says"—she had to go on—"that people should keep an open mind. Anything is possible."

"And how about you, Roger?" Mrs. Beckwith turned the corner toward Nina's street. "What do you think?"

"I guess I'd go along with . . ."

Dad? Dad was his stepfather. And she—she was his stepsister!

The next few moments were completely lost to Nina. She must have said the right thing in thanks, though, because everyone reacted very naturally as she left.

She stood still for a moment looking at the place

where the car had paused to let her out. Then a new thought gripped her, and she whirled to look at the garage.

Her mother's car wasn't there. Not yet.

Thank goodness.

 Chapter
14

All the girls Nina asked that Friday said they wouldn't be caught dead wearing a dress to the dance. They were wearing pants and as slinky a top as they could sneak out of the house in and, of course, all the makeup they could load onto their faces.

Although Merlaine had made a donation of eye makeup she never wore now that she was into the natural look, Nina didn't dare lay it on while her Mother hovered in the room.

The clothes fight was bad enough. "Darling, you're not serious! *That!*"

"Mom . . ." Deep sigh. "Everyone wears pants to a casual dance. It isn't like those freaky things you used to go to."

"I don't care for your attitude or your tone of voice. Why can't you wear at least one of the little skirts and sweaters Gram sent? They came from Saks!"

It was lucky Nina hadn't put on mascara. Her eyes were misting. "I'll just stay home then. That's all. I'll stay home."

"I give up. Wear what you like. Although when we get there and see the other girls . . ."

That was another thing. "You don't have to take me," Nina said. "Merlaine and some guy will drop me off on their way to rehearsal."

"I wouldn't mind. It would bring back memories."

"I doubt that, Mom. Things have changed. What are you going to do tonight?"

"My nails. Write a few notes. Talk to Phil if he calls."

"You going out with him tomorrow night?"

"Maybe. Maybe not. We had a little disagreement."

"What about?"

"You wouldn't understand. What time shall I pick you up then, tonight?"

"I'll call when it's over." Smarting from the *you*

wouldn't understand, Nina left the room. Let *her* try that when Mother asked questions!

She went down the hall and rapped on Merlaine's door to see if she was ready.

"Come on in."

Nina did and stared. She'd never seen Merlaine in anything but ill-assorted sports clothes or that bikini-nightshirt combination before, and here she was in a skirt. And what a skirt! "Where'd you get that thing?" she asked.

"Fantastic, eh?" Merlaine pulled at the material around an elastic waistband. "Wish I'd had a sewing machine, though. I'm not much with the hand stitchery bit."

The stitching was the least of it. "It looks like a bedspread," Nina sputtered.

"Aren't you sharp? It is. A madras number from India. I had it in one of the boxes to cushion my jars. It's done a lot of service. Aunt Merlaine used it as a tablecloth."

"And you cut it up."

"That's because the center was all cruddy from candlewax. From seances. I thought if I made a skirt from it it would help put me in the mood for the play at rehearsals. Catch?"

"It's kind of full, isn't it?" Nina said hesitantly.

"Yeah." Merlaine shifted some of the gathers to

the front. "This way I look pregnant." She shifted them to the side. "And this way broad as a barn door." She evened the gathers. "Oh, well. When I ramble off home tomorrow, I should find some good stuff. Let's go downstairs and wait for our ride."

Out on the porch, Merlaine leaned against a pillar. "What are the kids in your math class up to these days?"

"Nothing except trying to get farthest ahead in the book."

"Do they like the teacher now?"

"They always *liked* her. That had nothing to do with it."

Nina was hoping that even though the Accelerated gang had declared dances dumb, some would show up tonight so she wouldn't be alone. Angie had it all planned out how she was going to make a play for Craig. Nina would be on her own. What if Tom came up and talked to her? (He wouldn't.) But if he did, what would she do?

"Merlaine," she said, leaning against the opposite post, "what do you talk about at dances?"

"Talk? Who can talk above the racket? You just dance and don't ask questions." She started down the walk. "Here comes our ride."

Nina, now thoroughly confused, caught up and touched Merlaine's arm. "But what if . . . no one asks the question . . . and there you stand?"

"Then you amble up to some guy you know and say, 'Hey, clod, dance with me.'"

"Would you, really?"

"Of course. Girls have to take the initiative. Boys are relieved if you do, because basically, they're backward. At least, I've found that to be true."

Merlaine swung into the front seat and pulled her skirt over to make room for Nina. "Isn't that right, Ritchie?"

"That's right." Even though Ritchie didn't know what it was he was agreeing to, it was some consolation to Nina to have his support.

Inside the building, Nina was stopped by some unfamiliar man teacher. "Are you a pupil in this school?"

"Why . . . sure."

"Who's your homeroom teacher?"

"Miss . . ." the word *carrot* stuck in her mind. "Primrose."

"Hi, Nina." Mrs. Beckwith came from behind. "Imagine coming here from choice," she said with a grin, as they walked down the hall. "I got assigned."

"Oh. Well, maybe you can sneak out early," Nina said. "Or do they give detentions to teachers, too?"

Mrs. Beckwith laughed. "Where's Angie?"

"Waiting in the girls' room."

"I may go there later and hide out myself. Just listen to that . . . *music!*" With a little wave, Mrs. Beckwith entered the gym.

Nina hurried to the impatient Angie. "At last!" Angie shrieked. "Fix your face so we can get going. I've been here for hours because of Tom and his dumb committee chores."

"Is there much of a crowd?" Nina asked, leaning toward the mirror to darken her eyebrows.

"I don't know-oh," Angie said in an affected, accusing way. "I've been wait-ting."

"Sorry." Nina brushed on lavender shadow with a little sponge.

"That's sexy looking," Angie observed.

"Want some?" Nina held out the container.

"It doesn't show up on me. My eyelashes and brows practically meet. I hate it."

"Oh, sure. Lashes an inch long." Nina fumbled in her purse for mascara to darken and lengthen her own feeble lashes, but there wasn't any. A girl at the next sink let Nina borrow her gummy wand.

"See?" Angie piped up. "With makeup you look years older. I always look the same."

"Gruesome," the girl at the next sink commented.

Angie urged Nina to hurry it up. "Someone," she murmured, as they pushed out of the room, "is going to grab off you know-who if I don't get out there. By the way, who are you after?"

"No one." If she even hinted to Angie, she'd make so much of it she'd scare Tom off forever.

"Let's get a coke first and see what's going on," Angie urged. "I'll just die if 'C' is already dancing!"

He wasn't. No one was. The music from the super-amplified group bounced from the rafters of the gym. The floor seemed to shudder from the sound. Although the lights were dimmed and the committee had draped a few sick strands of crepe paper in autumn colors, it still looked like a gym.

"Take off your shoes," a student council member commanded. "The floor's just been refinished."

"Where should we put them?" Angie asked.

"Tie 'em around your neck for all I care."

Some goof-offs had done just that. Angie and Nina hid theirs under a bleacher.

Kids were talking loudly, but no one danced until finally a couple of teachers got out on the floor. Miss Gryce, the girls' gym teacher and Mr. Moore, the coach. "Look at that," someone said. Someone else hummed a few bars from the wedding march.

More teachers joined in. Mrs. Beckwith danced with a science teacher. Then an eighth-grade girl, on a dare, asked the principal to dance. Gradually, kids drifted out to the floor.

Buzz asked Angie. Probably just to make Cheryl burn.

Nina, left alone, drifted to a clutch of Accelerated

kids. It was okay for a few minutes until they, too, started pairing off.

She summoned up her courage and turned to Ken. "Hey, clod, want to dance?"

"Sure." Ken actually looked relieved. (*Merlaine, you did it again.*)

Once started, it wasn't bad at all. Time passed quickly. Now that she felt confident, Nina mixed with the kids and talked. It was past nine.

She was watching Angie, who was living joy, dancing with Craig. Someone tapped her shoulder. *Tom!*

"I really can't dance," he said, "but . . ."

"Okay." (I'd love to! Wow!) She started toward the floor and he followed.

"Really, I can't," he said. "I'm not kidding."

"But all you have to do is move to the music. See?"

He tried to copy her motions. No stranger could have guessed that this embarrassed, uncoordinated kid was the grace-in-action star of the basketball squad.

"You're doing fine," Nina lied. "All you need is practice."

Tom cast his suffering look toward the clock. "It's almost over," he said with some relief. "I made it just in time."

"What?"

"The coach said we had to. Just because he . . ."

"Likes the phys. ed. teacher?"

"That may be it. Well, so long."

"Wait." Nina wanted to ask, *And did you choose* me *because:*

    A. I'm your sister's friend and nobody special

            or

    B. I was standing there alone

            or

    C. I was the one you wanted!!!!!!

Instead, she said, "You shouldn't stop now." And wildly improvising, added, "You'll get a Charlie horse." All she knew was a Charlie horse had something to do with muscles.

Tom looked half convinced, and Nina got him dancing again before he had a chance to change his mind.

He was improving. "See?" Nina said. "You're doing great."

Tom's slow smile revealed that mouthful of metal. "You think so?" Then his smile faded and so did his steps. "Only I guess you have to leave. There's your mother."

"My mother!" Nina jerked around. There she was, standing at the entrance. "I told her I'd *call!*"

"The party's breaking up anyway. See you," Tom said. He walked with her just a few steps and then slipped away. Nina got her shoes, stepped into them, and stalked over to her mother.

"Darling, you didn't have to stop," Charlotte said. "I'd wait. Wasn't that the little Rafferty boy you were dancing with? He's grown so tall." Her mother reached to lift a sticky strand of hair from Nina's cheek.

Nina ducked. "Now that you're here, I'm leaving."

"Good heavens, Nina, you're so touchy. Are you ashamed of me?"

"Parents just don't show up." She started down the hall, purposely keeping ahead of her mother. Tom must think she was some kind of infant! She pushed through the door, not caring if it slammed, and was halfway down the sidewalk when she was stopped from behind by a clutch on her arm. She jerked her head, ready to dodge a slap, though she didn't deserve it.

Instead, her mother whispered, "George." She was round-eyed, staring ahead.

Nina followed that look. Dad! And he was walking toward them.

Before Nina could react, her father rushed forward and caught her up in a hug. "Nina . . . honey . . ."

"Dad." The pulse in her throat came like a panic warning. She couldn't think of what to say.

Her mother said it for her. With a voice more bewildered than hostile, she asked, "George, whatever are you doing here?"

He straightened. "I came to pick up my . . . pick up Dolores. And the boy." Nina hadn't even noticed Roger at the dance.

"Dolores?"

"I had to have the car, to go to a meeting."

"Oh . . . I see," Charlotte said.

She didn't see, at the moment. Nina could tell that by the uncertainty of her mother's voice. But she'd catch on soon enough.

After an awkward pause, her father said, "I'll call you soon, Charlotte, about any problems. And I'll see you tomorrow, Nina." He nodded and moved off toward the building.

Nina followed her mother to the car. She knew from the tight look on her face and the way she braked the car fast at every stop that she had suddenly understood . . . or at least suspected. But she didn't say a word.

When they got home, Charlotte stopped off in the kitchen. Nina hurried upstairs, hoping to get into bed and even pretend sleep before her mother came up.

She didn't make it. She'd just scrubbed off the last trace of makeup (which at least had not been noticed) when her mother walked into the bathroom with a glass of sherry. It must have been her second . . . and the first hadn't tranquilized her much, Nina decided.

"What was that woman doing at the dance?" Charlotte asked.

"Who? Oh, you mean . . ."

"She must have been there all evening."

"I guess so." Nina wet her lips. "I saw her when I first got there."

"Why was she there?"

"Well, Mom," Nina reached for her toothbrush. "She's a teacher."

"I know she's a teacher. But . . ." Her eyes were like blue spotlights. "You mean to tell me she's at your school?"

"Yes."

"How does it happen you've never once mentioned that little fact?"

At Nina's punch, the toothpaste squirted all over the brush. It was too late now to tell her mother in an offhanded way, so she just blurted out, "I knew you wouldn't like it. I . . . I have her for math."

"You . . . *what?*"

"I got assigned to her, Mother. And I hated it at first. But then I got used to it." As her mother stared, Nina fumbled, "She's really not so bad . . . I don't even think of her as . . . you know. She's just another . . ."

"You mean to tell me your father allowed this! Knowing!"

"He didn't assign me to that class!"

"But he did know about it. He knew, she knew, and you knew. It was only poor, dumb Charlotte who was left out in the dark."

"Mother!"

"Left out in the cold!" She looked strange and her voice trembled. Had she been drinking all evening? Nina wondered. It wasn't like her.

The phone started ringing in the room across the hall.

"Mother . . ." Nina said gently, "your phone."

Her mother paused, then turned, and left without hurrying.

Later, lying in bed, Nina tried to erase all the troubling things from her mind and relive those few moments on the dance floor with Tom.

She couldn't concentrate. And she couldn't fall asleep.

The phone kept ringing at intervals. So far as Nina could tell, her mother never did answer.

 Chapter
15

Surprisingly, the anger seemed to have drained away from Charlotte during the night. But judging from her looks, as she moved about, getting breakfast, she'd had a restless night. She's faded, like a picked flower, Nina thought.

"Mother, why don't you go back to bed?" she asked, with some concern. "I can walk to my piano lesson. I do when you have to work Saturdays."

"No, I might as well drop you off and do errands," Charlotte said. "I'll nap this afternoon when you're with your father." Nina gave her a quick glance, but there was no strain around her mother's mouth at the words. "Anyway," she went on, "I'm good and awake now. I took Merlaine to the Greyhound early this morning."

"Wearing *that?*"

Charlotte tightened the cord on her silk kimono. "Plus a light coat."

"What if you'd had a flat tire?"

"Oh, you worry-bug. Finish your breakfast." She sat with a cup of coffee opposite Nina. "Now tell me about this—teacher. Dear Dolores. How is she?"

"What do you mean?"

"Do you like her? As a teacher, I mean?"

"She's okay." Nina bit off a piece of toast. "Tough, but fair."

"What do you mean . . . tough?"

"She expects us to do the work, but she lets us go along at our own pace. When we come to something we don't understand, she always . . ."

"But you don't see her otherwise, out of class?"

"Well, no. She only teaches math and . . ."

"Is that boy of hers in any of your classes?"

"No."

"I'd better get dressed," her mother said, rising, "if we're going to get you to piano on time."

"Mother?" Nina tried not to sound alarmed. "You're not going to try to get me changed out of that room, are you?"

"That's something I'll have to think about. I ought to have been told. As a courtesy, if nothing else. Now, let's get moving."

She didn't mention it again, and neither did Nina.

When Charlotte drove up after the piano lesson, she seemed to have only shopping on her mind. "I picked up a sweater-top for you," she said. "To go with one of your blouses. And I'd love to take you back to try on a winter coat I saw, but we'd be late meeting your dad. It's a damned nuisance, these Saturday visits."

"Shall I call and say we'll be a little late?" Nina asked.

"Heaven forbid we should upset *his* schedule."

For the first time, her father was late. "I'm sorry, honey," he said, leaning over to swing open the car door. "Things are really in a mess today."

Nina, glad to get out of the chilling winds, started to scoot in, but stopped short. A little kid, scrunched down on the front seat, was staring at her.

"Oh." Her father's look shifted to the boy. "Climb in the back now, Paul."

"Don't want to."

"Paul!"

Protesting, the child crawled over the center shift, to the back.

149

Nina, scowling, slid onto the seat near the window. She picked up a stuffed animal by the leg and tossed it over her shoulder. She didn't look at her father.

"I'm sorry, Nina. Dolores isn't feeling well, and I have to pick up a prescription. Paul, this is Nina."

The child poked his head around the seat to stare right at Nina's profile. "Are you my daddy's big girl?"

Nina turned her face away to look out the side window. If the car hadn't already been moving, she'd have gotten out.

"Sit down, Paul, please," Mr. Beckwith said. In an undertone, he said to Nina, "He put up such a howl when I started to leave I was afraid he'd awaken Dolores. She was up half the night."

She felt a hand on top of her head. "Pretty," the little voice said.

She jerked around and glared at him. The boy's eyes widened. He scrambled onto the farthest corner of the back seat.

Nina glanced at her father. She could see that vein throbbing at his temple, a sure sign he was distressed.

"Is she . . . very sick?"

"No. One of those sudden stomach things. It just came at a time when I'm loaded with all kinds of extra work." He blinked away at the fatigue. "How are things going with you? Anything new in the worm department?"

"No, but Merlaine's in a play. *Blithe Spirit.*"

"I've seen notices around the building. What character is she?"

"The medium."

Nina turned toward the soft sounds in the back seat. Paul was sobbing into the worn fur of his stuffed animal. He really was a baby. "Does he cry at everything?" Nina asked her father.

"I'm afraid so. Roger left for basketball practice this morning, and I wouldn't let Paul disturb his mother. So he's feeling sorry for himself."

Nina glanced around again. He did look pathetic. "Come on," she said. "You can sit on my lap."

Silently, with a big fat tear streaking his cheek, the little boy came forward and settled against her with a sigh of contentment.

"You should be quiet at home so your mommy can sleep," she said. "And get well."

Paul pulled away and stared at her with large wet-lashed blue-gray eyes. He didn't look anything like Dolores or Roger. "You like Paul Lee?"

"Sure, I like you," Nina said. "What's this Paul Lee business?" she asked her father.

"Pauly is his baby name. But you're becoming a big boy now, aren't you, Paul?"

The child chattered away while Mr. Beckwith was in the drugstore getting the prescription. He stayed on Nina's lap during the drive home and, once there, refused to budge unless Nina went into the house with him.

"Come see my toys and play with me," he insisted. "For a while. A little while."

Nina laughed at her father's look of exasperation.

"I'll come along to keep the peace," she said. "If that's okay."

"I'd appreciate it, Nina," her father said. "I know this is supposed to be our time together, but I really should stay a while just to be sure Dolores is all right. And see that she gets started on this medication."

"What shall we play, Nina?" Paul asked, digging his knees into her as he reached for the door handle.

"Don't expect her to entertain you all afternoon," Mr. Beckwith said. "We're leaving as soon as Roger gets home. And you're taking your nap."

"No nap," Paul said. "Carry my bear. Carry it, Nina."

"Carry it yourself," she said. She took his hand and followed her father into the house.

Wow . . . was it ever small! She'd never pictured him in a place like this, not after the big, rambling Beckwith house.

"Come see my toys," Paul insisted, pulling at Nina.

"Let her get her coat off first," her father said. He put his own in the closet by the front door and handed Nina a hanger. "I'll be right out." He went through the living room and to a door just beyond.

Nina knelt to help Paul with the button at the top of his zippered jacket and then looked around at the cramped living room. The furniture seemed to be survivals from Dolores' first marriage, except for a new-looking recliner chair. The only familiar thing was an heirloom pedestal table that had once been in their front hall. Oh . . . and Dad's desk. It used to be in that room of his own, his study. Now it was jammed into a corner, overflowing, as always, with books and papers. And there were her photographs . . .

"Nina!" Paul pulled at her arm. "Come look at my toys!"

She leaned down and, shifting Paul's foot, removed his jacket from the floor and hung it up. "Let's go."

She followed him to a room so small it had bunk beds. "Do you share this room with your brother?"

"That's Roger's bed." Paul pointed to the top bunk. The wall was covered with sports pictures and a couple of *Mad* posters.

"And that," Paul said, pointing, "is Roger's desk. Don't you touch that desk, Nina."

"Why should I?" She stepped forward, though, and looked at the things belonging to the strange boy whose life had got mixed up with hers. Nothing very interesting, except for the beer-can lamp.

Paul was watching her solemnly, hands behind his back. Roger had probably cracked him a couple of times to make him leave things alone. "Where are your toys?" Nina asked.

She and Paul were sitting on the floor putting together a circus puzzle when her father came to the door. "That must be miracle medicine," he said, looking relieved. "Dolores feels better and she hasn't even taken it yet."

"Good."

"She even feels hungry."

"I want Mommy." Paul juggled the puzzle out of place.

Nina put her arms around him.

"I guess he could go in for a minute," her dad said. "But Paul, no jumping all over the bed."

In the kitchen, her father started tea, toast, and a boiled egg. "We'll leave in a few minutes," he said.

"Dad, where will we go?"

"I don't know."

"It's such a lousy day outside. I wouldn't mind just hanging around."

He shot her a glance. "Are you sure? Look, you're under no obligation."

"Neither are you, to entertain me. Can't we just be together?"

With her father's arms around her, she said, "I'll even fix lunch."

Paul burst into the room. "Daddy, you forgot the glass of water for Mommy."

"The classic absent-minded professor."

Nina was opening a can of soup when Roger burst in through the back door. "What are you doing here?" he asked.

Paul rushed to him. "She didn't touch anything. I said, 'Don't touch Roger's desk!' "

"Nina's helping," her father said. "How did practice go, Roger?"

While they talked, Nina assembled the tray. It looked so blah. She dashed outside. The garden, such as it was, had only a few scraggly button mums. Poking around, she did find one blossom with a little color. She took it inside, along with a leaf spray.

"You have your mother's instinct for beauty," her father said, as she put the flower next to the silver. "Want to take the tray in to Dolores?"

Because of Roger standing there, Nina didn't want to remind Dad that women hated to be seen when looking sick. She took the tray to the partly opened door. "Mrs. Beckwith?"

"Nina? Oh, please come in."

Dolores was propped up, reading the label on a plastic bottle of pills. "What a lot of gibberish this is," she said, looking up and smiling. "I'm going to take a course in prescription deciphering. Hey, what have we got here," she said, putting down the bottle and making room for the tray. "How dandy! You can tell there's a girl in the house."

For an awful moment Nina thought of the daughter-who-had-been, but from the looks of Mrs. Beckwith that wasn't in her mind. "George told me how sweet you've been with Paul. He says you've charmed him. You'll have to slip me the secret."

"He's cute," Nina said shyly.

"He's a bad actor. Sit down for a minute. I'll try not to breathe in your direction. This looks good."

Since there was no other place to sit, Nina perched on the edge of the bed. "Are you feeling better?"

"Lots. Sleeping all morning must agree with me."

Except for being a bit pale, she didn't look bad at all. Her hair, being short with natural curl, didn't need fixing, and her eyes didn't have a faded look since she never wore makeup anyway.

Dolores dipped the tea bag into the hot water. "Did you enjoy the dance last night?"

"Some." (Up to when her mother had appeared.)

"Roger said you're a good dancer."

"I didn't dance with him!"

"Of course not. He's too shy. Too shy to learn, even."

"So was Tom." Nina fought not to blush. "Angie's brother. But I got him to dance."

"If Tom did, then Roger could be persuaded," Dolores said. Paul came bounding into the room. "And if this fireball can be persuaded to fizzle out this afternoon . . ."

"Paul, you'll nap for Nina, won't you?" she coaxed.

"No."

"Let's help Dad . . ." Nina caught herself. *My dad* she wanted to change it to, but looking at that solemn face, she couldn't make the words come out. "Let's go put lunch together," she said, getting up. "And then we'll see."

It seemed natural now to take his hand. And to smile at Dolores, as though they'd always been friends together in this house. Out in the kitchen, even Dad no longer seemed out of place, puttering around.

What had happened, anyway, in just one hour? Was this some kind of enchanted cottage? If so, Nina was perfectly content to be under its spell. At least for today.

 Chapter
16

When Dad drove her to her real home late
that afternoon, they saw a car sitting in the driveway.
"Hey, Phil must be here," Nina said.
"Phil?"
"Mom's boyfriend."
"Oh?"
"*Man*friend, I mean. He's not exactly a school
kid." Nina wished she hadn't said anything. Since Dad
made no comment, she continued, "Mom sees Phil
once in a while. Just to break the monotony."

"Nina, you don't have to explain. It's your mother's prerogative."

"Yeah. Well, 'bye, Dad. See you next Saturday, and I'll call during the week."

He kissed her. "It's been a very good day for us. I hope it has been for you."

Nina wondered what kind of day it had been for her mother. The two of them—her mother and Phil—were sitting in the living room drinking coffee. Phil stood politely when Nina paused at the door.

"Come in, lamb," her mother said. She gave a slight twitch to Phil's wrist, and he sat down again.

"I'll just go up . . ." Nina began.

"Come sit by the fire," her mother urged. "It's so deadly outside. We nearly froze."

"Froze!" Phil laughed. "The only time I came to was when we walked through the parking lot. What an afternoon!"

"You mean she dragged you shopping?" Nina sank to the floor in front of the fireplace. "I pity you."

"Oh," Charlotte said, "but wait until you see the chiffon number I picked up. And on sale, too. Admit it, Phil, the effort was worth it."

He laughed again and shook his head. "It beats me how women can go on, hour after hour . . ."

"And in a shop in this town," Charlotte interrupted. "I never dreamed I'd find anything that chic out here. I guess that's why it was marked down. Phil, you really do like it, don't you?"

"Love it." The kidding smile as he looked at her mother slowly faded, and a different kind of look took over. Nina turned toward the fire. She wished she could leave without being conspicuous.

"Since you're so run down, then," her mother was saying to Phil, "I'd better feed you a steak and salad before you start back. We wouldn't want you to collapse in the middle of the highway."

"Nonsense. I'll take you both out to dinner."

"I thought you had to see friends tonight."

"I guess I don't, after all."

Nina supposed that whatever they had fought about had been forgotten. "I'll stay here," she said.

"I'd like you to go with us." Phil turned to Charlotte. "If it's all right with you."

She shrugged. "Great. Where shall we go?"

He named a place Nina had never heard of. Her mother looked pleased. "Then go get changed, pet. A dress. Something nice."

A *dress*. Unwillingly, after a feeble protest that didn't register, Nina went upstairs and got ready. She'd rather stay home all alone than go out with them. *Him*. Even though Phil (the pill man) didn't seem as phony-polite as the first time she'd met him, she didn't want to be stuck with him all evening. He was just being friendly to her to please Mom. She bet once they got to the restaurant he'd order drinks and let her sit there like a dope for hours.

She was surprised, then, when Phil told the waiter they'd simply have wine for the meal and wanted to order at once. She was surprised, also, to see in this first-time nearness that Phil wasn't so magazine handsome after all. The pinkish light of the little table lamp, which turned her mother into a glowing goddess, brought out the lines in Phil's long face. Her father had worry lines in his forehead, but Phil's, along his mouth, seemed to be laugh lines. He laughed a lot, and said some things Nina didn't understand, but he didn't seem to be doing it on purpose. A lot of the talk was about what went on at his job. He was some kind of sales manager, whatever that was.

Looking at him, Nina marveled at how Phil seemed to bring out the best in her mother. And then she couldn't help thinking of Dolores and how Dad always looked so relaxed around her.

On the way home, sitting in the back seat by choice, Nina didn't pay much attention to the bantering conversation up front until her mother uttered a soft "shhhhh."

"Oh, Char, come off it," Phil said. "Don't you think Nina knows what it's all about?"

"I don't think children should grow up too fast."

161

"They usually grow up when they're ready."

Instead of being annoyed, her mother teased, "Why haven't you?"

"I'm not ready," Phil said.

"What do you think?" Nina asked Merlaine late the next night. As usual, they had sneaked down to the kitchen for a getting-through-the-night snack.

Merlaine had picked up a new hard-boiled-egg-and-banana kick at home over the weekend. "Think about what?" she asked, shelling her third egg.

"About Phil."

"From what you've told me, he sounds okay."

"But I wonder what he and Mom had the fight about. Before."

"Ask her."

"She wouldn't tell me. She doesn't talk about things like that. Not to me."

"Then ask him." Merlaine showered the egg with salt.

"Him! I've only met the guy twice."

"Kid, I can't see that it's all that important." Merlaine bit off about a third of the egg, taking in some yolk. "Now, if they got married—"

"Married! They hardly know each other!"

"Remember, you were gone all summer." Merlaine pinched up a piece of yolk from the table.

"Anyway, what am I supposed to tell you? You'd think I was psychic."

"That's what you say."

"I'm off duty. You coming to opening night of my play? It's this Friday, remember."

"I guess so."

"Guess so? You'd better be."

"When arc we going to have that seance you promised?"

"Sometime. I can't clutter up my mind right now."

Looking at the egg shells and banana skins on the table, Nina hoped Merlaine's mind was neater than her eating habits.

It was cold the Friday night of the play, but Nina was burning. "We're going to be late, and we won't get good seats, and I promised we'd be up front . . ."

"Quiet," her mother said calmly, turning the key of the ignition once more with a kid-gloved hand. This time the motor caught.

"You always complain," Nina grumbled as they backed out, "about my tying up the phone. And you . . ."

"But it was business. I have to go into the office tomorrow. It's going to be a big day, with someone in from New York."

163

"Oh." Nina wished she'd known that before. Mom could have stayed home and rested up. And she could have gone to the play with Dad. And Dolores. Only the last she'd heard, they were still trying for Saturday night seats.

When Nina and her mother finally arrived, the play had begun and the auditorium was nearly full, but they found places over to the side. On stage the husband and wife were beginning to talk about Madame Arcati, the medium. Nina, shrugging out of her coat and getting settled, felt a nervousness for Merlaine, waiting backstage to make her entrance.

She needn't have been nervous. Merlaine wasn't. Or at least, she didn't appear to be. Wearing a red and purple caftan and trailing some kind of feather boa, Merlaine created an air of excitement that renewed itself each time she made an appearance.

"I want to go backstage and see her," Nina told her mother after the play. "Merlaine said I should. She said she'd introduce me to the director and to the girl who plays the ghost-wife. Please? I won't be gone long. Or . . . you come, too."

"I'd rather not." Her mother's eyes were shadowed under the small brim of the black velvet hat. Her pearl earrings glowed. "I'll wait here. Don't be long."

Nina scooted past people, pausing only to flash a smile when an occasional faculty member called to her. She hoped Mom wouldn't get stuck talking to someone she couldn't stand.

Merlaine wasn't easy to get to, there was such a jam of college kids backstage screaming congratulations.

It wasn't worth the effort. By the time Nina got through the crunch to Merlaine, the girl-ghost was at the other end of the room. A quick hug and a "how'd you like it?" and Merlaine was grabbed at from another direction. Nina edged out of the mob scene (whew, it reeked of makeup!) and into the hall.

Her mother wasn't by the pillar. Looking around and short-cutting through a row of empty seats, Nina headed up the center aisle. A voice, topped with carrot hair, said, "Hello there, Nina."

"Miss Primrose. What are you . . . oh, Dolores!"

"Hi, honey." Dolores, looking snappy in red plaid, came away from the clump of women. "Your friend was great."

"Thanks. Is my dad . . . ?"

"He was called out of town on some administrative thing. So I popped over with Ellen." She glanced at Miss Primrose. "Seats are sold out for tomorrow night anyway."

"Oh." Nina glanced around nervously. Where was Mother?

"I tried calling you this evening, but your phone

was tied up. Your dad won't be back until some time in the afternoon tomorrow, so he asked me to pick you up. Is that all right?"

Nina barely nodded. She'd just seen the black-velvet-and-pearl glow of her mother in the lobby. And her mother had seen her. " 'Bye, then," Nina called over her shoulder to Dolores as she hurried up the aisle.

"Put on your coat," her mother said, and started walking.

"I'm sorry," Nina said, trailing along, buttoning herself against the wind. And then, inside the car, shivering in the cold stillness, she explained, "All she said was that Dad's out of town, so she'll pick me up tomorrow."

She couldn't understand her mother's silence. She's tired, Nina finally decided. And thinking about her job.

When they reached the kitchen her mother paused. "Call her and tell her not to bother."

"Wh . . . what?"

"I'm taking you with me in the morning. To the office."

 Chapter
17

"I don't see *why* . . ." Nina wailed the next morning, as her mother scribbled a note to the still-sleeping Merlaine. "Why can't I go there?"

"I still have custody," her mother said, not looking up from writing, "and if neither he nor she has the courtesy . . ."

"She *tried* to call last night, but you had the phone tied up!"

Since that got no reaction, Nina went on, "What about my piano lesson?"

"I've canceled it. Come on. And on the way, wipe

off that eye shadow. I told you to look like a lady, not a budding harlot."

In the car, dabbing at her eyelids with tissue, Nina said resentfully, "Pauly is going to be disappointed. But I suppose you don't care about that."

"Who's Pauly?"

Nina looked up, surprised. "My little . . ." She caught herself. "Dolores' little boy."

"Oh, so it's *Dolores* now." Her mother swung onto the main highway.

"What do you expect me to call her . . . *Mother?*"

"Just keep this up, Nina," Charlotte warned. "You never used to use that sulky tone. What is it, that they let you do whatever you like over there?"

"You know Dad better than that."

"I used to. Now I'm not so sure." After a pause, in a quieter tone, her mother said, "Nina, please help me. This is an important day. Mr. Johnson himself is flying out from New York Monday, and we have to have all our fragrance research ready."

Why, Nina wondered, did she have to be dragged along then? It was just jealousy. Mother didn't want her to be with Dolores.

"Today," her mother continued, "we have to pull everything together because they say Mr. Johnson always shows up early." She put on a pair of huge dark glasses. "I hope he's impressed."

"Why?"

"Why?" The sun glanced off her lenses. "Because it's my job. And I want to be good at it."

With those words, her mother seemed to withdraw from Nina and project her thoughts to the office. It was like riding with someone who looked the same but had suddenly become a stranger. Even when they arrived and rode up in the elevator together, her mother seemed to be a great distance away.

"Good morning, Mrs. Beckwith," the young woman at the reception desk called out. "Oh . . . something important."

"Yes? Laura, this is my daughter Nina."

"Hello, Nina. Mrs. Beckwith, Mr. Johnson is here."

"Here? Now? Good lord, you're kidding."

The young woman lowered her voice. "It threw Mr. Moore, too. He got a little call from the airport. And there they were."

"They?"

"He brought along Mrs. Johnson. She's at the hotel. *He*'s in there." Laura motioned down the carpeted hall. "Having coffee. Waiting for you. I tried calling, but you'd already left." Laura turned to answer the switchboard and then lifted the earphones. "Shall I tell them you're here?"

"Give me a few minutes to pull things together." Charlotte started off, and Nina followed her to her office.

"Are you worried, Mother?"

"Not worried, just caught off guard." Tossing her things into an empty chair Charlotte hurriedly assembled a stack of folders. "I heard he's eccentric, but this . . ." She picked up the ringing phone. "Yes, Laura, tell them I'll be right there."

"What shall I do?" Nina asked, bewildered.

"Oh. Well, find something." Her mother, with a glance in the mirror on the wall, left.

Nina swiveled in her mother's desk chair and looked around. The office was all business, with file cabinets and stacks of stuff everywhere. The only Charlotte things were a rose in a crystal bud vase, a china sugar server, which held pencils, and a silver-framed photo of Nina. Ick . . . at the age of four.

Find something, her mother had said. Like what?

Since it was only an office desk, Nina went through all the drawers (boring, except for some perfumed stationery) and then, with just a touch of guilt, leafed through the desk calendar. The only interesting thing, among all the notes, was a reminder of lunch with Phil.

"How are you doing?"

Nina jumped. It was Laura.

"Want to come out and keep me company? I'll show you how to run the switchboard. Oops!" Laura took off at the sound of the buzzer.

Nina followed and for a while sat on a stool and

170

watched. There was so much going on, with calls and people running back and forth, that she never could figure out the workings of the snakelike setup.

"Sir," Laura said, at one call, "I'm sorry, but she's in a meeting and can't be interrupted. May I take a message?" Pause. "Oh, yes, Mr. Nelson, I'll see . . . oh . . ." Noticing Nina's interest she added, "Mrs. Beckwith's daughter is here. Would you care to speak to her? Just a moment, please." She murmured to Nina, "Pick up the phone in your mother's office."

"Phil?" Nina said a moment later. She hoped Laura wasn't listening in. "I came down with Mother today, but she's all busy because of some man from New York."

"Do you think she'll be tied up for lunch, then?"

"I don't know."

"All right. Ask her to call me, sweetie. Maybe we can get together later."

As long as she was at it, Nina decided to phone Dolores. She didn't care if it *was* a toll call. Laura gave her a line and told her to go ahead and dial.

Roger answered. "Thought you were gone today," he said. "Mom's not home."

For some dumb reason, Nina felt let down. "Where is she?"

"At the barbershop. With Paul."

"Oh. I'm at my mom's office. And I was just wondering what everyone was doing." Since Roger made no reply, Nina said a feeble good-bye and hung up.

What difference should it make to her what Dolores and Paul were doing? Dad was the only one who mattered. She swiveled some more in the chair. Would Paul cry when he got his hair cut? Bet he wouldn't if she were along. She'd charmed him. That's what they'd said. He was so cute. One of these days . . .

"Hi." A woman with streaked hair and black-rimmed glasses smiled from the doorway. "Want to see our display room, Nina?"

Nina obediently got up.

"Your mother asked me to show you around. I just came from the meeting. This is our showroom," the woman said, as they entered a room that had the hushed elegance of a Michigan Avenue jewelry store. The woman moved along the lighted showcases, with perfumes displayed like gems on pedestals.

"Are these all new?" Nina asked.

Judging from the woman's laugh, it was a dumb question. "These lines have been established for years. They're world-famous. It's terribly expensive to bring out a new fragrance."

"Oh."

"And if it doesn't go over . . ." The woman shrugged.

After that one question, Nina hated to say anything else, but she couldn't stand there like a stupe, either. "Who decides?" she asked. "On the new fragrance?"

"I guess the people in Paris. But we have to come up with a good strong suggestion backed by research. Have you tried our samples? No? Come, we'll test them out on you."

She took Nina to a room that seemed to be all cardboard displays and bottles. There were three boxes on the table, each containing dozens of tiny vials.

"Hold out your wrist," the woman commanded. She dabbed a few drops from a number 1 vial and waggled Nina's hand. "Let it dry," she said. Then she put drops from the other sets on Nina's other wrist and on the inside of her elbow. "You always put it on the pulse points," she explained.

They all smelled the same to Nina. Strong. Before she had to make a choice, the woman was called away.

Back in her mother's office, to kill time, Nina took out some perfumed stationery and practiced drawing Tom's initials with hers. She tore the paper to shreds and then started a note to Angie on another sheet. She'd die when she smelled it.

"Oh, baby . . ." Her mother finally swept in, flushed but pleased looking. "Are you bored out of your mind? I hear Phil called. Wow, what a session."

"You're supposed to call him."

"Charlotte?" A voice called from the hall. A man appeared. "Are you sure you don't mind . . ."

"This is my daughter, Nina. Nina, this is Mr. Moore."

Nina stood up and shook hands with her mother's boss.

"Charlotte, if it's going to be complicated . . ." he said, holding Nina's hand but looking at her mother.

"No, no. I'd have to go home anyway to dress."

"Well, I certainly appreciate it." He let go of Nina's hand and looked at her. "I don't know how we'd get along without your mother."

After he talked to Charlotte about a few more business details, Mr. Moore left.

"He's tied up tonight," Nina's mother explained, dialing for an outside line. "And asked me as a big fat favor to go out to dinner with the Johnsons. Oh, just pray that Phil agrees. I could never manage it alone."

Half listening as her mother talked to Phil, excitement still coloring her face, Nina realized for the first time in her life that her mother, free now, on her own, could probably do anything. Grownups *did* change, sometimes. And that was good. But it was also a bit unsettling.

"It's a long ride, isn't it?" Nina said, as they

battled the Saturday afternoon traffic. She felt sleepy from lunch and from the perfume that seemed to seep right through her coat to permeate the car.

"I'm getting used to the drive," her mother said. "Sorry we have to rush back like this."

"Will Phil pick you up tonight?"

"Yes, poor dear. Way out there and back. But he's so good-natured. He never complains."

Nina took a long look at her mother, so different from the sometimes listless, sometimes resentful woman she'd known for the past year or so. She must dread this drive every day, back to the run-down monster of a house she hated so much. And once again Nina wondered if Mother really would consider selling it. Should she ask? Or leave well enough alone?

Finally, taking a deep breath, she began, "Mother, would you . . ."

"Slow down? Okay. But I *am* in a hurry. Do you suppose you girls can manage dinner alone tonight?"

"Sure."

As her mother made suggestions, Nina fell silent. This, obviously, was not the time for a serious talk.

Although Merlaine offered to take *the kid* to the play and stash her away somewhere backstage, Nina declined. She knew how she'd be ignored in all the wild commotion and be bored.

"Do you want Angela to come over to keep you

company?" her mother asked, fastening on earrings and giving Nina a concerned look.

Nina flopped on her mother's bed. "They have company. I could"—she hesitated—"go over to Dad's."

Her mother's hand paused a second and then continued with the earrings. "They're not to be used as baby-sitters, Nina." She went to the closet. "I could call Mrs. Walters, down the street, to come stay with you."

"I'm not afraid! And I'm too old for a sitter. I'll just . . . hang around."

"Oh, darling." Her mother cupped Nina's chin and gave her a fast kiss on her way back to the dresser. "You *are* growing up. We're going to be such good companions. Now, where did I leave my beaded bag?"

"There." Nina stretched out a lazy arm. "On the chair under your robe." She sat up. "Mother, if you've really faced the fact that I'm not a little girl, would you do me a favor?"

"Such as?"

"Put a different picture of me on your desk. I'm not that girl in the silver frame."

For a moment her mother paused—like that stop-action thing they did sometimes on TV. Then she leaned toward the mirror. "Okay," she said. "But I don't know how I'll keep up with you. You're changing every day."

After the noise and confusion of Mom's and Merlaine's leaving, the sudden silence of the house surrounded Nina. I'm not afraid, she thought, double-checking the doors. There's nothing or no one out there to hurt me. She triple-checked.

She looked at the phone in the kitchen and thought of calling someone. But a voice without that person was not the answer. The house seemed almost to say, *It's you and me, now, Nina.*

As though pulled by an unseen thread, she wove her way through every room on the lower floor and then through the hall and up the stairs. She looked into her mother's room. In spite of Charlotte's rush, she'd put everything in place, so that without her presence it was a picture room in a magazine.

Next, Merlaine's place. A tumbled heap that could be cleared in tornado time, with nothing left to show she'd ever been there.

Her father's one-time office, now with odds and ends, was like a rebuke.

Nina didn't go into her own room. There was time enough for that. Instead, she went to the front of the house to her once-beloved turret room, and here she sat in the middle of the floor.

What had happened? She didn't know.

So many people, so many things, pulling at her in all directions. What was she supposed to do? What was she supposed to feel?

My life, she thought, has been split in half. I don't know which way to turn.

Her thoughts flowed toward the little house where Dad lived now. Although it was small and over-crowded, there was room for her there in that warmth. But not for all the time. She belonged with her mother.

But did she?

"Mother, I want to know you," Nina half whispered. "I want to be part of your life, to share. Can't you see that?"

"We're going to be such good companions." That's what her mother had just said. But how could that happen? How could Nina make her mother realize that companions were more than two people living in the same house?

A sudden wind rattled the windows. Nina shivered. She raised herself to her knees and the thought came. Perhaps there *were* spirits in this house. In this room. The place had always belonged to a Beckwith. And she was a Beckwith. Could those spirits help her now?

If she sat there silently, waiting, could they send her a message? Just a friendly little something-or-other?

She waited. Nothing happened.

Finally she arose and went to the door. As she reached for the switch, she got it. A memory-message. The seance! Of course, the seance!

178

Merlaine had said the minute she stepped into this room that she'd felt something strange about it. And weird as she was, that girl did have certain insights.

So, wow! They'd have the seance. And see if the spirits had something to say.

Whether they did or not, Nina thought, going to her room, it should be an interesting evening. She'd start working on Merlaine and make her set a date.

Chapter 18

"It's all right with me, duckie," Merlaine said, looking up from her books when Nina approached her the next afternoon. "In a couple of weeks, okay?"

"A *couple!*"

"Well, maybe sooner. Remember, I need time to decelerate from the Madame Arcati role and become myself again. To say nothing of knocking out a couple of midterm papers and studying for exams. I *am* supposed to be a student, you know."

"But that's so long to wait!"

"Don't just wait. Do something. Get some candles together. And some stuff to spook up the room. Decide what kind of message you want to receive and then try your best to empty your mind."

"What about Angie?"

"That mind is already empty."

"I mean, what should she do?"

"Help you get ready, for all I care. And she can help me the night of the seance by keeping her mouth shut and stifling the giggles. If that's possible."

"What kind of message do *you* want to receive?" Nina asked.

"I've already received a message. From the dean's office, about my grades. So scram now, will you?"

It wasn't easy, but Nina waited until Angie came over after school the next day to spring the news. It was a good thing. Angie practically howled with excitement.

After she quieted a little, Nina cautioned, "Now whatever you do, don't say a word to your family. My mom, of course, doesn't know. And don't you dare tell anyone at school!"

"How come?"

"It's supposed to be secret and spooky. You know how Buzz is, with his scientific questions. He'd ruin the mood with his talk-talk-talk."

Angie agreed. "Once Buzz gets tuned in, he just

doesn't stop. As you so well know. But can't we get started on something? Like make a list?"

"Okay." Nina got a sheet of paper from her desk, and they sprawled on the floor.

After a little arguing, they settled on the items:

1. Clear a space in the turret room.
2. Cover stuff we don't need with sheets.
3. Set up a date.
4. Find something to make a magic circle. (No marks on the floor.)
5. Get incense. (Merlaine has some.)
6. Make candles.
7. Think about message.
8. Get symbols.

"What do you mean, 'get symbols'?" Angie asked, as Nina wrote that one down.

"Merlaine said we should have something solid for the spirits to lay hands on."

"I don't want any crummy spirits laying hands on Craig," Angie protested.

"*Craig?*"

"He's what I want to receive a message about. How to get him to like me."

"Oh, really!"

"What's wrong with that? Just because *you* don't like anyone! "

Nina bent over the list to hide her face. Not *like* anyone! If Angie only knew!

"What's your message going to be?" Angie asked, unaware. "Something far out?"

"No." She thought of her mother. "Something near."

"Like what?"

"I'd rather not discuss it." Nina ran a finger down the list. "We have eight items. We ought to have seven. Seven's a mystic number."

"Cut out number three," Angie said. "That's not really doing anything. It's just a matter of nagging that klutz Merlaine to get with it. And, of course, finding a night when your mom's not home. Any idea when that might be?"

"Nope." Nina got up on her knees. "Let's start clearing the turret room for action."

"Right. I'm all charged up with nervous energy."

Since Angie already had a kit, they decided to make candles at her house.

"We've got a problem," she said the day Nina came over. "I couldn't find black dye anywhere. Do you suppose we could melt down some licorice?"

"We don't want black anyway. Merlaine said to keep away from anything witchy."

"Why?"

"She's going to try to contact her Aunt Merlaine, who went for gaudy colors."

"And who didn't take baths," Angie remembered. "I hope she's aired herself out a little if she pays us a visit. How many candles do we need?"

"Three. One for each of us. If our flame goes out, that means . . ."

"Don't say it!" Angie screeched. "I'm getting goose bumps already!"

Nina lined up three candle forms and got Angie busy melting wax. "If I were you," she said, "I'd kind of cool it the night of the seance."

"In what way?"

"I wouldn't kid around too much. Merlaine might be a little jumpy about trying to make contact with her aunt. It's been a long time since they met." And also, Nina thought, if any spirits *should* come drifting in, they'd probably be Beckwiths. Kindly, but not much for monkeyshines.

"You're shaking now," Angie said. "What's the matter?"

"This wax is hot. Watch out, I have to pour it." Nina did. "It isn't enough," she said. "Do you have any old candle stubs we could melt down?"

"I'll ask Mom," Angie said. "Let's put these in the freezer to hurry them up for the next layer."

The two girls found Mrs. Rafferty in the doll room with one of her reference books.

"Mom," Angie said, "are there any old candles we could have? We need wax."

"Wax?" Mrs. Rafferty's hand went out protectively to a doll sitting nearby.

"Oh!" In a teasing tone, Angie said, "I didn't think of her!"

Mrs. Rafferty gave a nervous laugh. "And you'd better not. I'm almost sure she's a genuine Montanari. Do you know how rare these dolls are?"

"Not rare enough," Angie said, with a look at Nina. "They're still around."

Nina leaned forward to touch the doll's cheek. "If it's really wax, why hasn't it melted?"

"She's had excellent care." Mrs. Rafferty pointed to a photograph in the book. "This one was made in England in the year . . ."

"Oh, Mom . . ." Angie protested.

"Hey, Mom," Tom called from the door.

All three turned.

"Do you remember finding a glove when you cleaned my room?"

"I don't remember cleaning your room," his mother said with a vague frown. "Did you lose a glove?"

"Craig did, and his Mom is burned. She's laying it on him because it was a brand new pair. Genuine leather."

"You stay here," Angie said, patting her mother, who had given no sign of stirring. "I'll help look." She darted from the room.

Feeling terribly ignored, Nina dropped into a chair next to Mrs. Rafferty. As she half listened to an account of the manufacture of the marvelous Montanaris, Nina shuffled idly through a box of tiny dolls.

"Are these valuable?" she asked, during a pause.

"Not very," Mrs. Rafferty said. "I bought that boxful at an auction because of one doll in it. I'll try to sell the rest somewhere. The one you're holding is a Frozen Charlotte."

"Really? Why is it called that?" Nina stared at the tiny figure. "Because it's so stiff looking?"

"According to the book"—Mrs. Rafferty reached up for another reference—"they were named for an old Vermont ballad, called 'Fair Charlotte'."

"Charlotte is my mother's name," Nina said.

Mrs. Rafferty ran a finger along the index. "Here it is." She turned to the page and handed the book to Nina. "It's about a young woman who froze to death because she was too vain to wear warm clothes." She went back to her own book as Nina read:

> *Fair Charlotte lived on a mountain side,*
> *In a wild and lonely spot,*
> *No dwelling was for three miles 'round*
> *Except her father's cot.*

She skipped through several verses of description to the one where a young man came to take Charlotte for a sleigh ride:

Her mother said, "My daughter dear,
This blanket 'round you fold,
For 'tis an awful night without,
And you'll be very cold."

"Oh, nay, oh, nay," young Charlotte cried,
And she laughed like a gypsy queen,
"To ride in a blanket muffled up,
I never will be seen."

Then the ballad went on to tell how the two of
them rode through the frosty night in the sleigh, and it
kept getting colder and colder. By the time they
reached the ballroom, Charlotte didn't stir. And then:

He took her hand into his own,
Oh, God! it was cold as stone!
He tore her mantle from her brow,
On her face the cold stars shone.

Then quickly to the lighted hall,
Her lifeless form he bore,
Fair Charlotte was a frozen corpse.
And her lips spake nevermore.

"That's very sad," Nina said, pushing the book
aside. (Also, she thought, a bit slurpy.) "I wonder if it's
true."

"True or not, that's how the doll got its name,"
Mrs. Rafferty said. "You can have her if you like."

"Oh, thanks." What would she *do* with it? Happily, Angie came bursting back into the room.

"Tom couldn't find the glove," she said, with a guarded look on her face. "Where are the candles, Mom?"

"Look around. In the buffet? I don't know."

When they got back to the kitchen, Angie grabbed Nina's arm and, glancing around to be sure they were alone, whispered, "I have it."

"You have what?"

"His glove. I found it yesterday."

Nina pulled back. "Didn't you tell him?"

"No. Tom talked to him on the phone. Darn, I thought Craig was here."

"Angie, why do you want to keep his glove?"

"It's something of *his*. For the seance. A symbol."

"That's rather mean. Keeping the glove when his mom's mad."

"He'll be all the more grateful later, when I 'find' it." Angie headed out of the room. "I'll look for the candle stubs and you check to see if that first layer's hardened."

Starting to open the freezer, Nina realized she was still clutching the two-inch doll. Not knowing what else to do with it, she shoved it among the stuff in her purse.

The wax, she saw, was congealed, so she set the forms out for the next layer.

188

Looking around the kitchen, she wished she could find something of Tom's as a symbol. All she saw was a milk glass he hadn't rinsed out. But even if she found something good that was his, she couldn't use it. Not with Angie there.

Besides, romance wasn't the reason for having this seance. At least not *her* reason.

She was reaching for something. But what? Warmth? A kind of *big-kid* security blanket?

"I found them," Angie said, coming into the room, her hands cupped with candle stubs. "In this family we've always saved everything."

As Nina stooped to pick up a candle that had fallen to the floor, she thought, In our family we never saved anything. We didn't even save the family.

 Chapter
19

The turret room was cleared, ready for the right night.

On Wednesday morning, a wonderful thing happened. Merlaine told Nina they could set up the seance that same week.

"Your mother asked if I'd be around Friday night to protect you from the wolves and wild beasts. She's going to be out until dawn breaketh. Or at least 1 or 2 A.M."

"Wow!" Nina exclaimed. "I'll tell Angie. She'll flip."

It was shivery, waiting at the bus stop. Winter was already on its way. Nina thought fleetingly of poor Craig, with one cold hand.

She sat on the last seat and waved Angie back. "The seance is set for this Friday. Can you sleep over?"

"Of course!"

"Let's get the candles from your house after school and start lining everything up. I found an old hanging lamp in the garage. We can use the chain to make the magic circle."

Angie gave a shudder of delight. "Craig won't even know what hit him when he gets in my power. And the timing is just right. There's going to be a holiday dance at school in a couple of weeks."

"How do you know? Oh. Tom."

"He actually asked me to practice dancing with him last night. Tom, I mean. Isn't that a riot?"

"Did he say why?" Nina asked.

"I guess he thinks if he has to go, he might as well make the most of it. He said you're a better dancer than I am. I told him to get you to teach him, then."

"You didn't!"

"Oh, he won't. He'd be embarrassed. Now, don't let on when Metal Mouth asks you to dance."

To cover her confusion, Nina murmured, "You shouldn't call him that."

"I don't always. Sometimes it's Brace Face, Tinsel Teeth . . . can you think of any more?"

"No. If he were *my* brother . . ." Nina didn't finish. She was glad he wasn't.

Angie, sniffling slightly, rooted around in her purse. "Do you have a Kleenex?"

Nina dug into her shoulder strap bag. She pulled out a tissue. A little object rolled onto her lap. The doll. Again, no place to get rid of it without notice. She pushed it back in and took a tissue for herself. The cold season was starting early.

"You haven't told me," Angie said, flipping her hair, "what you want the spirits to do for you."

"I'm still thinking about it," Nina said, which was true enough.

At about eight o'clock Friday night, Nina suggested to Angie that they pop corn just to kill time. They were too excited to settle down.

"Should we go up and ask Merlaine if popcorn is all right?" Angie asked.

"She said not to disturb her. Besides, popcorn is a grain. What's wrong with that?"

"I feel sorry for you. Cheese sandwiches for dinner. What did your mother say?"

"She's eating out," Nina said.

"Couldn't you have had hamburgers and aired out the kitchen?"

"Merlaine said absolutely no meat."

"Her aunt's probably gotten over being a vegetarian by now. Death is a different way of life. How soon's your mother leaving?"

"At about nine, she told me. Oh, look, it's snowing. You can see it by the porch light."

"Darn!" Angie said. "I was wishing for a bleak, barren Halloween kind of night."

"Snow can be spooky, too," Nina said. "We're really getting an early winter."

"That's all right with me. This batch of popcorn is done. Hurry up with the butter."

Later, up in Nina's room, they munched while listening to records.

"I'll go see if Mother's about ready to leave," Nina said finally. She hoped her mother wasn't wearing a certain something.

She was.

"Is anything wrong?" Charlotte asked, looking up from her nails. She turned for a swift look at herself in the mirror.

"I was just . . . wondering why you're wearing those earrings."

Charlotte gave a light laugh. "Don't I always, on big occasions?"

"But . . ." Nina felt confused, not knowing how to say it. "Doesn't Phil mind? I mean they used to belong to Grandma Beckwith."

"Why should he mind?" Charlotte waved her nails in the air. "Besides, baby, diamonds are diamonds. Some day they'll be yours."

Nina didn't want to think about things like that.

She sat on the edge of a chair and bit her lips. If Mom wore those diamonds tonight, she would have to do some quick replanning.

After a lot of thinking, Nina had finally seized upon a symbol for the seance. Those very earrings. She'd been delighted when she thought of them. After all, didn't some people call diamonds "ice"?

What could be a better symbol than those cold, glittery diamonds . . . the very ones Dad had given her mother before their wedding? Now, if she, Nina, used those earrings and concentrated during the magic moment, maybe Mom would thaw a little toward her and take her into her confidence.

It's not so much the *future* I'm worried about, Nina thought, as just not being *told* things. Mothers and daughters ought to be able to . . .

"Nina?"

She gave a little start. "Do you need some help, Mom?"

"If you'd get out my dress and unzip it—the new white chiffon."

Nina brought it out. "It's awfully skimpy. On top."

"And the velvet evening coat." Her mother tested a nail. "Dry at last."

"Why don't you wear the black velvet dress? And the pearl earrings?"

"Because I want to wear this. Don't nag, Nina." Her mother got into the dress and adjusted the thin straps. "Really, don't you think it's divine?"

"What there is of it."

"There's Phil," her mother said, as the doorbell rang. "Would you let him in? I'll be right down."

"Hi, Nina," Phil said a moment or two later. "Brrrr, it's cold. But a beautiful night." His eyes lifted to the stairs as Charlotte descended in a swirl of white. "*Very* beautiful. Hi, angel." He kissed her lightly.

"Honey," Nina's mother said as Phil helped her with the long wrap, "don't you girls stay up all night with your chitchat."

"Not all night. Have a good time," Nina called, as she went up the stairs. "Don't freeze," she added, as a blast of cold air rushed up from the opened door.

Even though there was no rush—Merlaine had said *under no circumstances* to disturb her before a quarter to midnight—the two girls hurried to the turret room the minute Phil's car pulled away.

"These sheets aren't white!" Angie said, taking up the stack Nina had hidden.

195

"So? Merlaine said no witchy-spooky stuff, remember? I even wish we had something brighter than pastel. But the candles are wild, at least."

The girls formed a circle of the chain and set the candles in a triangle within it.

"That's it," Nina said. "Merlaine will bring the incense."

"Shall we put out our symbols?"

"Not yet." Nina had to think of an alternate to the earrings—and fast. "Let's watch TV in Mom's room. Maybe there's something scary on." And she might see something in the meantime that she could use.

"Just a minute." Angie joined Nina, taking something out of her purse. "Here's Craig's glove. I'm going to wear it for a while to get some warmth going. You might as well tell me what your symbol is. I'm going to see it anyway."

There must have been a spirit in the room. Why else, seeing Angie's purse, would Nina suddenly have *known*. "Okay."

She came back with her own purse and took out the Frozen Charlotte.

Angie stared at the little figure. "A doll? Have you gone into your second childhood like my mother?"

Nina explained about the name and what she hoped would happen. The skeptical look on Angie's face vanished. She looked at the doll almost with awe. "Frozen Charlotte. Perfect."

Hugging herself, Angie said, "I have this feeling in my bones. Tonight's going to be a smash!"

 Chapter
20

Since there was nothing scary on TV, the two girls sat in the dark, reading a story of the supernatural by flashlight. They finished with five minutes to spare. Even so, tense and ready, they jumped at the sound of the tap on the door.

"I'm scared," Angie said, clutching Nina.

"Stop that." Nina shook her arm away and rose to open the door. She didn't feel so steady herself.

The hallway was dark except for the faint light coming from the candles in the turret room.

"It is time," Merlaine said in a hushed voice. "You will follow me."

She looked very strange. Nina, sensing giggles about to erupt from Angie, gave her a sharp jab in the ribs.

They walked into the room and seated themselves cross-legged on the floor, each behind a candle.

"Place the symbols," Merlaine said, indicating a position near the candles. Before her, she had a script book from *Blithe Spirit* and next to it—ugh—Joey, bobbing around in his jar.

Through the haze of the incense, spinning upward from the center of the circle, Nina saw that Merlaine was wearing the tablecloth skirt she'd made, a black top, and that bedraggled feather thing from the play draped around her neck. Her hair was almost hidden by a fringed scarf. She had a gaunt look from gray eye shadow on her cheeks and all around her eyes. Her nails, painted green, looked like moldy rose petals. She clasped an old Mexican jug and solemnly closed her eyes.

"Before we proceed . . . are there any questions?" Merlaine intoned.

A moment of silence. Then Angie piped up. "I have one. What's that thing you're wearing around your neck?"

Merlaine's eyelids snapped open. "A chicken

feather boa," she said in a perfectly normal voice. "Why do you ask?"

"It stinks."

"It does not stink. It was a prized possession of my dear, departed aunt."

"That figures," Angie said in an undertone. "Do you have to wear it? I'll bet it's crawling with lice." She started scratching her arm.

"The discussion is closed," Merlaine said sternly. She blew on the incense. When the smoke cleared and they'd all stopping coughing, she continued: "We will now meditate on the Great Beyond. I will endeavor to summon the spirit of my beloved relative, now passed over, in order to bring her great strength and wisdom to bear upon the problems of the present. We will pass this magic potion and sip from it and then fall into great meditation. *Silent* meditation.

"Should I feel the presence of my darling Aunt Merlaine, I will signal this by putting before her the problems which beset me. You will then follow, in counterclockwise order."

Merlaine sipped from the jug she was holding and passed it to Angie. Then Nina took a sip. Hawaiian Punch with what—catsup? She almost gagged.

Now with those moldy-green fingertips against her forehead, Merlaine closed her eyes. She began rocking softly from side to side. Her low humming sound became a mumble and a croon and then finally words:

> *Auntie . . . Auntie show your face*
> *Enter here from . . . outer space.*

Nina didn't dare look at Angie, who had said, under her breath, "On a UFO maybe?"

Merlaine was too far out of it to pay attention. She continued:

> *If you're with us, give a sign.*
> *Blow the candle, sip the wine.*

Wine. That was stretching the imagination. Nina could still taste . . . oh! The flame of Merlaine's candle was flickering. She darted a quick glance at Angie and then at Merlaine. Neither seemed to have noticed. But then, their eyes were closed.

Nina kept her eyes on the Mexican jug. *If the liquid level starts going down, I'm getting out of here.* No. That's why we're doing this.

But nothing more seemed to happen.

Merlaine reached out her arms, signaling that they should all join hands.

The three of them began swaying slightly, while Merlaine mumbled stuff that had no meaning. Then:

> *Come within this magic trance . . .*
> *Join us . . . uh . . . join us . . .*

Angie piped up, "Before I wet my pants?"

"Really!" Merlaine snapped their hands loose. "What do you think you're doing?"

"Just trying to be of help. Besides, I do have to go."

"Time out," Merlaine said, with a disgusted look. She took up the jug to take a sip and then thought better of it.

When Angie rejoined them, Merlaine said, "Now listen, guys, we can't keep this up all night. My powers of concentration are being overtaxed. Get with it and stay with it from now on, okay?"

She started in on some high-powered mumbling then, but didn't relapse into any more of her punk poetry. Nina's mind began wandering back to the night she'd been home in this room. *Alone?*

"We will now meditate," Merlaine announced. She pressed her fingertips to her brow once again and motioned them to do likewise. They did.

Merlaine's flame started flickering. They all noticed.

"Auntie, I have placed these symbols before me," Merlaine said in a solemn tone, "so that you may guide me with your other-worldly wisdom. Joey, here," (she touched the jar) "is a symbol of my ambitions in the veterinary field. While this play book" (she touched it) "indicates another ambition—to be a star of the stage. Which, in your wisdom, do you think it should be? For me?"

Nothing happened.

"We will give beloved Aunt Merlaine time to check through the fate files," Merlaine said, in what appeared to be a wild inspiration. "Proceed, Angela."

"I have here a glove." Angie pulled at her lips to keep from laughing at this obvious statement. "It belongs to . . . to someone I like. I hope he likes me. So could you give him a little nudge?"

Angie turned to Nina.

Nina wished she had never started this. She felt self-conscious and also . . . afraid.

Merlaine fixed her with a look.

"I have here," Nina began. "I have here a . . . Frozen Charlotte doll. I want my mother to . . . to thaw out. And . . ." She looked up helplessly. "That's all."

"You have heard our requests and our desires," Merlaine said. "Have you an answer, O Wise One?"

At that instant a gust of cold air burst into the room. The candle flames flickered and went out.

There was the sound of Angie's intake of breath, a scuffling, and a dull plop.

"Turn on the light, someone," Merlaine said in an agitated voice. "Something's happened."

Nina felt on the wall and flicked the switch. Joey's

jar had cracked, and the liquid was soaking the edges of the play book.

Merlaine grabbed the jar. "Looks like Auntie wasn't wild about either idea! Nina, run get some Kleenex! There, there, Joey, you're all right. Mommy's here."

Nina brought back a box of tissues from her room and tossed it to Merlaine. Neither Angie or Merlaine seemed to notice that Nina went back into the hall, closing the door after her.

What was downstairs? Something. She had known it the instant the candles blew out.

Now, standing at the head of the stairs, she stiffened with terror. She remembered the words of the ballad:

Then quickly to the lighted hall,
Her lifeless form he bore,
Fair Charlotte was a frozen corpse.
And her lips spake never more.

What had she done! Such a cold night. And snow! And her mother . . . her mother in that thin chiffon dress and velvet wrap! The Charlotte doll had been meant as a warning . . . not as a symbol for the seance!

Teeth chattering and breathing huge gulps of air, Nina clung to the banister and slowly, softly descended.

She rounded the curve. The faint hall light glowed.

And there was the mirror. Something stirred . . . something white. Nina could see it in the mirror, faintly, like a mist.

Her mother. Her mother and someone else.

Nina's eyes widened. She peered over the banister.

It was her mother all right. Very much alive. Phil was kissing her, and not at all lightly this time.

Nina sank down onto the step.

So Frozen Charlotte wasn't frozen after all. She had thawed all right. But not in the way Nina had intended.

It was at least two hours later. Phil was long gone, Charlotte was apparently asleep, and Angie was snoring softly. Nina's thoughts were like carnival rides, dipping and swooping and jarring her more awake by the minute.

At a familiar sound across the hall, she went to the door. "Merlaine? You going downstairs for a snack?" she whispered.

"Of course. Come on."

In the kitchen, Nina watched Merlaine heat the usual warm milk to cushion her stomach for the main event. "Did you hate the way the seance turned out?" Nina asked.

"No, Joey's all right."

"*Joey!* I meant, nothing *happened.* So you still don't know what you ought to be."

"You must be kidding." Merlaine chuckled. "I wouldn't stake my future on some hocus-pocus parlor game. Even if we'd been serious about the whole thing. Want to join me in my diet?"

"We're out of eggs."

"That's okay. I'd as soon switch to salami sandwiches."

Nina went and put bread in the toaster. She felt letdown and a little foolish. "I know it was just for fun," she admitted, "but I couldn't help thinking that . . ."

"Thinking *what?*"

She shrugged. "I couldn't help hoping if I sort of believed in friendly spirits . . . in this house . . . they'd show me a way to thaw out my mother. But it didn't work out that way at all. In fact . . ."

"Why did you call that little doll Frozen Charlotte?"

" 'Cause that's its name," Nina said shortly.

"Oh. So it worked out well as a symbol. Personally, though, I don't think your mother is all that cold."

Nina thought, *That depends on which way you mean.* She took the bread from the toaster. "Of course, she's not *cold.* But she's not a person you can open to and tell what's on your mind. I ought to know. I've tried."

"Maybe you haven't tried hard enough," Merlaine said, slicing the salami.

"I *have!* You just don't know!" Oh, why waste time talking about it. What good would that do?

"You open up to your dad, don't you?"

"That's different. He listens."

"So would your Mom, I bet, if you really put out the effort."

"Huh!" Nina glared as Merlaine sloshed mustard onto the sandwiches.

"I'm not saying she'd spill her innermost thoughts, just like that . . . whoops!" Merlaine paused to scoop splattered mustard from the table-cloth. "But gradually, she'd start giving answers to what's bothering you. I know she would. Just try."

"How do *you* know what's bothering me?"

"I don't know *what,* exactly, but I know it's connected with your mother. You said so yourself, at the seance. And again, here, just a minute ago." Merlaine sawed through the sandwich with the dull knife. "So—make up your mind. Keep on brooding about it or do something. Here's your sandwich. Eat."

Nina got up. "I'm going to bed."

"What about your sandwich?"

"Eat it yourself."

"All right, I will," Merlaine said. "For breakfast."

 Chapter

21

Happily, considering the way Nina felt the next morning, Merlaine wasn't around. So the three of them—Angie, Nina, and her mother—ate a normal type of breakfast.

Ordinarily, Nina would have considered it a treat, having Angie there, but today, determined to break the ice with her mother, Nina felt impatient.

"I thought you had to be home by nine," she remarked to Angie.

"Nina!" her mother protested.

"It's only eight-thirty," Angie said, not one bit insulted. "That was a blast last night, wasn't it?"

"It was okay."

"I don't mind about your having a seance," Charlotte said, checking the cupboards and making a shopping list, "but you girls must not have had much sleep afterwards. Nina, you look washed out."

"She was really into it," Angie observed.

"I was not!"

"Oh, no? You were white as a sheet." Angie pushed away from the table. "Especially after you came in from the hall. Who did you think was out there anyway, Dracula?"

"Oh, leave me alone." Nina walked to the door and stood, as a not-too-subtle hint.

Angie got it. "I guess I *should* be going. 'Bye all! Thanks for breakfast and everything." With a wave, she grabbed her jacket and took off.

"Nina," her mother said, "that really was rude."

"Angie doesn't care. Anyway, I'll explain later."

"I wish you'd explain to me now," her mother said. "Is something bothering you? Or don't you feel well?"

This was it. The perfect opening. It was on the tip of Nina's tongue to say, "It's *your* behavior that's bothering me." Instead, she mumbled, "Where's Merlaine?"

"Merlaine? Upstairs, vacuuming. For heaven's sake, can't you hear it?"

"Oh. I forgot."

Her mother went back to the shopping list.

Nina thought, What if she wants to marry Phil, but she's afraid even to mention it? Because she doesn't know how . . . *she doesn't know how to approach me, either!* Nina swallowed hard. All these years she'd gone to Dad with her troubles, and Mother . . . Mother hadn't been included.

"I can't understand why we always seem to be out of eggs these days," her mother said. "I swear, last week . . ."

"Merlaine ate them all for her diet . . ." There was a catch in her voice, and as her mother glanced up, Nina burst into tears.

"Honey, what is it?" With widened eyes, her mother went swiftly to Nina and put a hand on her shoulder.

". . . to lose weight," Nina finished, tears spilling onto her cheeks.

"Goodness, that's nothing to cry about. We can afford eggs." Charlotte felt Nina's forehead. "I think you have a touch of fever. Nina, do you feel sick?" And before Nina could answer, "What *really* went on here last night?"

"We told you. A seance." Nina brushed at her

cheeks. The tears stopped and she got control of her voice. "That's all. A seance."

Charlotte slipped into the chair next to Nina. "But Angie said . . ." She frowned. "What upset you? It must have been *something*."

In the silence, Nina suddenly knew she had two choices: She could brush it off as Angie's imagination or she could blurt out the truth. Nearby she heard kitchen sounds and from upstairs a sudden loud clang of the vacuum cleaner and what sounded like a few choice swear words.

"Won't you tell me, Nina?"

In another moment it would be too late.

"Mother," she said. "I saw you kissing Phil last night." She looked straight at her. "Downstairs, in the hall."

Her mother blinked. She moved her lips slightly.

"And I wondered," Nina continued, "what is going on."

"Nina . . . really . . ." Her mother looked like a butterfly, ready for flight.

"Please! I don't mind!" Nina burst out. "I don't. But you see, I have to know. I mean, you're my mother!"

Her mother's lashes beat like tiny wings. "But, baby . . ."

"I'm not a baby! That's just it! I'm a person, and

I ought to know what's going to happen in my very own life!"

Her mother looked at her and Nina looked back. They had never looked at each other in quite that way before.

Charlotte glanced down then at her intertwining fingers. "Yes, you have a right to know," she said. She looked up again to meet Nina's gaze. "But I don't know myself. I honestly don't."

"You don't know if you love Phil?"

"Oh, Nina, it's not so simple as that."

"Why not?"

"To love someone. There are so many ways of loving."

"Have you thought of marrying him?"

"We've discussed it. But there's no rush."

"If you did . . . if you did marry Phil, would you move to the city?"

Charlotte twisted her ring.

"And take me with you?"

"Nina, so many questions all of a sudden . . ."

"Would you?"

"*If* I married Phil and *if* we moved to the city, you'd be with us. On that, there's no question."

"But Dad . . ."

"Honey, those are things we'd have to work out." She looked at Nina. "All of us. This time. You see, I have to be sure that . . ." Her voice faltered, but her look said it for her. It was both pleading and bewildered, like that of a child. No, not like a child. Like a mother who needed her child.

Nina could hardly trust her own voice. "I know," she said. She could feel the barrier between them beginning to melt. After a moment, she got up and touched her mother's shoulder. "We'll work things out." In the silence she didn't know what else to say. She started to leave.

"Nina?"

She paused.

"I know I've been busy. And it may seem I'm not concerned. But I am."

"I know that."

"It's just so hard for me to realize you're not a little girl any longer. That you're someone . . ."

"To share things with?"

"Yes. But also someone I have to share." Charlotte gave a little smile. "Isn't it strange? I feel closer to you than ever before. Yet I realize that little by little I've got to let you go. *Isn't* that strange?"

"Yeah." Nina shrugged. "But I guess that's life."

Her mother laughed and stood up. "My little philosopher. Sometimes you remind me of your father."

"And he says I remind him of you."

Charlotte looked pleased. "But you're really yourself."

"Mom!" Nina gave a big grin. "See, you're changing, too. Or you'd never have said a thing like that." She leaped toward her mother and gave her a hug. "I've got to get going now." She whirled off toward the door.

"Wear something warm."

"Okay. But nothing fits."

"Then let's go shopping after your lesson. Oh! I keep forgetting . . ."

"We could go some evening next week," Nina suggested. "Hey, we could even take Phil along. Show him what he's in for if he marries us!"

To the sound of her mother's laugh, Nina raced toward the stairs. She felt weightless, as though with a leap she could rise to the very top. It was like one of those super-happy dreams of flying.

Upstairs, Merlaine came padding down the hall.

"You're going to cream me," she said. "Know what I just did?"

"What?" Nina asked, her thoughts still suspended.

"I ran the vacuum over this and smashed it." Merlaine fished doll fragments out of her shirt pocket. "Your Frozen Charlotte. Sorry, kid. It was on the edge of the runner and I didn't see it."

"Oh."

"I'll get you another, but you'll have to tell me where."

Nina looked at the crumbled pieces. "That's all right, Merlaine. I don't want the doll." Was it only last night she'd looked upon it as a symbol? "I don't need stuff like that any more."

Merlaine gave her a look. "Something's happened. Good news?"

Nina didn't want to talk about it. Not yet. "It's one of those days. You know?"

"Sure do. Sun and everything. Guess I'll finish up here so I can go out and catch a few rays."

"If you'll leave the vacuum out, I'll do my room later."

Merlaine nodded, dropped the doll pieces into a wastebasket, and went back down the hall.

Nina stepped into the turret room, which had been freshly cleaned. The windows were open. She took a deep breath. The pure, winter-fragrant air seemed to swirl inside her. For a moment, breathing deeply, eyes closed, she could almost believe the Beckwith spirits were wafting a benediction. "I'm part of you," she whispered.

She opened her eyes.

There would be moments of heady happiness like this. And there would be moments of near misery. Nothing stayed the same.

She went to the window and kneeling, leaned on the sill. Even now, the tree branches were releasing their last fine traces of white. Clouds were drifting into the blueness of the sky.

In a little while Dad would be driving up. And sometime later Phil would be dropping by. Separate, but now both a part of Nina's life.

And perhaps some time . . . Tom. It was possible. All sorts of things were possible.

"Nina?"

She turned at the sound of her mother's voice from downstairs.

"Are you almost ready?"

Nina stood up. "Almost," she called.

She *was* almost ready. For anything.

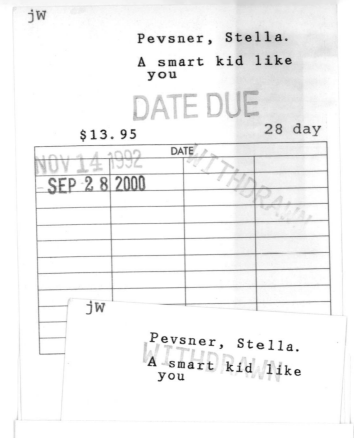

Redwood Library and Athenaeum

Newport, R. I.